# Journey South

## A Screenplay

Journey South
Alan Marcus

ISBN-13: 978-0-9629909-3-9

Please address all queries, comments, and requests for further information to OtherShorePress@prodigy.net

# JOURNEY SOUTH

A Screenplay by

ALAN  MARCUS

*333 Central Park West NY 10025*
July 1972

*Dear Alan:*
*....About "Journey South"·····/ think it should be in print well as on*
*the screen ....It's already rhythmed and finished as prose and*
*the quality of feeling and beauty of language, might well be lost*
*on film unless it were in the hands of a master. It sums up the*
*whole mood of the sixties. And as writing····in my view---it's too*
*good in itself to be left to the anonymity of a movie script,*
*because it's not only a guide or tool for a director,*
*but a completed art work of its own...*

---- Pauline Kael
(Chief movie Critic for The New Yorker--1968--1991)

\*\*\*\*▲\*\*\*\*\*\*\*\*\*\*\*\*\*\*\*\*\*\*\*\*\*\*

## *By Way Of Introduction*

****

The saga of the screenplay you're about to read really begins the day that I broke my self-imposed rule about getting involved with "complicated" ( i.e. "serious" )subject matter in my hit-and-run career as a screenwriter for the movies. I had come to Hollywood in 1949 as an invited author of prize-winning fictions, ---and saw writing for film a good way to subsidize my profound commitment to the art of prose --- having learned that - in the majority of cases,-- the General Motors assembly line model of filmmaking --which Hollywood pioneered,------------(and prospered from!) ---pretty much means that the pervasive confusion-- or collision between "Art" and Commerce---- which runs like a Wagnerian leitmotif through many aspects of mass film- making, -- is apt to be trumped sooner or later by the pluses and minuses of The Bottom Line; thus, anyone foolish enough to take seriously the ongoing rhetorical (off-stage) palaver one tends to keep hearing about the unexploited "potential" of film as a medium to plumb the "enigmatic" depths of human experience etc..-is eventually going to hit a brick wall, as I witnessed, firsthand, more than once, .........In my particular case, I certainly DID work (under a pseudonym) on some favorite projects of various producers now and then, in both film and television --But on the whole, I simply found it more congenial to my temperament to follow a freewheeling (figurative) surfboarding life as a free lance, where, if you weren't able to reach success (i.e. pay dirt!) on any particular try, you could always try again.

However, at just about this time, ----providentially ---- I happened to receive notice that I'd been awarded a year's Guggenheim Fellowship as a <u>novelist</u>,---with enough funds to allow me to write whatever I wanted & go wherever I felt like to write it ...!.... So presently my whole family ---my -wife, Lotte, and our three small kids ---went off, happily to Mexico, where we'd never previously lived ----, and before long, I was happily pursuing my lifelong addiction to the art and beguilements of fiction (which I had never quit working at, even while siphoning money from Lotus land to pay for the family groceries...)

Which is how it happened that --,some months later,-after we were happily ensconced in San Miguel D'Allende, in the state of Guanajuato, Mexico in what was called "<u>/a mesa central</u>' ( the central plain) I happened to pick up a copy of an overseas edition of The New York Herald Tribune one day and saw, staring me in the face, a scary headline about a serious tanker collision off the coast of Santa Barbara, California, causing a huge oil slick, now polluting the pristine waters off Santa Barbara bay; this event triggered a huge brouhaha in the media which suddenly rediscovered imminent dangers to our natural environment from various and sundry sources.. Indeed, -for a brief time---the term E-CO-LO-GY -now became enshrined in the national vocabulary. And this word ---which had been under-emphasized ----despite various previous prophets hitherto howling, in the wilderness ---suddenly became a tocsin of daily warnings & preachments - popping up everywhere -----on Editorial pages, in media talk shows, in Congressional debates, and in Presidential press conferences..

So -it wasn't too long before, ----lo and behold !----<u>Journey South"</u>, my "failed" nuclear accident piece, -------previously rejected by every studio in town!---- suddenly turned, overnight---into a "hot" property! People began flirting with me about it, telegrams and notes began arriving ...from entrepreneurs I never heard of, and especially urgent ones from my agent who shall be called "Robert" in this scenario

*"Please call me, I have a firm offer from blah blah blah on a screenplay for "Journey South.../ can't reach you, vital we stay in touch. Etc etc.. !*

Although reluctant to tear myself away from my new manuscript which seemed to be going well, I eventually listened to my wife's urgings and made the call. And it developed that "Robert" wanted me to come to LA to meet the two principles who'd made the offer on "JS.".

Both were prominent director-producers, it turned out, (each with a prior Academy Award statuette to his credit) And since I had nothing to lose but a few day's work, I agreed to a meeting....To my great surprise, when I got there, I learned they didn't want to follow the simple suspense story line of the original anymore! They were now interested (they said) in *"enlarging its stature"* (which is pure "movie-speak" for spending more money on it... (i.e. translation: stuffing it with more expensive Stars!), thus adding more "class" to the whole project, automatically converting it into a "prestige" production, --and potentially even a viable candidate when Academy Award time came around again.

The drama of what happened next -two or three months later - when I sent back a finished screenplay ----is not so important as what happened to me when I got back to San Miguel, my Mexican home town. In a word, --despite my own sound advice,--- I fell off the wagon!...You may remember my previously saying that the Bottom Line not only rules---it often dismembers ----the fate of many erstwhile "thoughtful" movies in Film Land, and that the better part of wisdom is to throttle whatever "significance-mongering" impulse threatens to creep into whatever script you may be writing ....But when I got back to Mexico, I suddenly

6

realized that I was all *alone* in the middle of nowhere! No faxes, no motor-cycle messengers, not even a truly dependable long distance telephone line!---*("Free At Last!"*, as Martin Luther King once famously said!) -Furthermore, armed with the implicit encouragement given me by my erstwhile employers about *"Journey* South"-(enlarge its stature," they'd said,)—I disregarded my own rule, and decided to go for broke on what could be a really far-reaching film -----converting what had been a professionally taut suspense melodrama into something deeper and far more reverberating by imagining a highway accident between truck and car which cause several drums of radioactive waste to fall from the truck in to a nearby rural area, leaking a small amount of potentially lethal cargo here and there. Which forced me to try to imagine the kind of affects such an accident might cause, not only the original cast of characters, but various other people they were destined to come in to contact with – a chronicle of increasing and often contradictory responses amidst all the cries raised by the nuclear accident itself. At the same time I became interested in trying envision a new kind of sound track that might employed kind of "contrapuntal" commentary to what was going *visually,* instead of blandly underlining --or "hyping up"-- the action on screen ----- with music cloned from fragments purloined from the classical repertoire, often the usual "default" way of employing it. .The eventual result, though, was what my friends and well-wishers back in the States all began warning me was a film altogether too "European" for American tastes....The film critic of the *New Yorker*, however, Pauline Kael, ----whom I'd known since we'd both appeared in the same Cal lit magazine decades earlier ---- informed me in a written note that what I'd actually put down, in fact, whether I knew it or not, was

*"...a kind of "movie novel", as well as a screenplay ...it's already rhythmed and finished as prose and the quality of feeling and beauty of language, might well be lost on film unless it were in the hands of a master....It sums up the whole mood of the sixties. And as writing-----in my view---it's too good in itself to be left to the anonymity of a movie scrip because it's not only a guide or tool for a director, but a completed art work of its own...."*

7

The most astonishing response came, initially, from my two academy--award winning employers who responded with an exuberant long-distance phone call, congratulating me on how much "better" than the original the final draft had turned out, how much more "significant" and "important", a movie it now was, how it might even turn out to be an actual contender one day when Academy Award time rolled around...

Something should've warned me, of course, that the "final" word had yet to come. And when it *did* come, ----via another long distance call about three weeks later ----it confirmed all my original misgivings about just how precarious it was to mistake working on a film assembly line for an artist's atelier.

*This* time ,the voices of my twin sponsors were definitely subdued; they told me the "score" ,on their efforts so far to secure funding for our mutual project had definitely not been -urn--- *"encouraging"*----------*i.e.* they had gotten 3 straight turn downs in a row ! .... I remonstrated: well, three turn-downs was surely not the end of the ball game?... Yes, they said, wearily ----- under the circumstances, it *really was---the "end of the ballgame!"* ... When I asked *why,* they explained that, for one thing, the town (Hollywood) was right then going through a very "dry spell".... Warner Bros, Paramount, Fox--- all were momentarily "dead" when it came to funding new projects...And the industry was very "strange"----if word should get around that three major Studios had already "passed" on *"Journey South"* , the property might become a little "tarnished" in the eyes of others.. .. Well, what did they expect me to do, then, I asked,,?....,It seemed that what the project needed, one of them delicately suggested, was more of what he called *"audience-grabbing"* material....,Because the critiques that came back---although acknowledging the excellence of the writing itself, (no question!)_---------said it was felt by most readers that the script was MAYBE a little too "poetic" and PERHAPS too much *"over the heads* of people..." But if I could come to LA right now and "put back" a little of the *original* suspense & melodrama that had been in the *first* version -(the version they hadn't wanted, remember?) -- in other words, add enough jolts of *"audience grabbing"* material" to it!--- perhaps these reluctant investors might be turned on enough to cough up the required amount of dough to get a production started

**The only way I can adequately describe the kind of 180 degree turn-around they were now requesting of me, is to quote one of Kenneth Patchen's late poems which goes like this:**

### IN ORDER TO

Apply for the position (I've forgotten now for what) I had to marry
the Second Mayor's daughter by twelve noon.
The order arrived three minutes of.

I already had a wife; the Second Mayor was childless: but I did it.

Next they told me to shave off my father's beard. All right.
No matter that he'd been a eunuch, and had
succumbed in early childhood: I did it, I shaved him.

Then they told me to bum a village; next, a fair-sized town; then, a
city; a bigger city; a small, down-at-heels; then one of "the great
powers"; then another (another, another)-

In fact, they went right on until they'd told me to burn up every man-
made thing on the face of the earth! And I did it, I burned away every
last trace, I left nothing, nothing of any kind whatever.

Then they told me to blow it all to hell and gone!
And I blew it all to hell and gone (oh, didn't 1!)...

Now, they said, *put it back together again;*
*put it all back the way it was when you started.*

Well... it was my turn then to tell *them* something!
*Shucks, I didn't want any job that bad!*

---Kenneth Patchen

The result, of course, was that I was forced to do the only honorable thing left to me; I regretfully resigned from the project, leaving them free to hire a bunch of new "audience-grabber" experts ,-to assure themselves of getting the required production funds .....But, alas, none of these feverish efforts panned out, either ........Although , ironically enough, ,I found myself soon receiving sporadic notes from several of these newly hired "audience-grabber" virtuosos , praising my own script highly ,and hoping it would be adequately produced one day ....After the officially designated time had elapsed, naturally, the legal "rights" reverted to me, But I didn't ----or couldn't, --- for various reasons ,want to have anything to do with it anymore at the time.

Nevertheless, *"Journey South"* ,-- which I recently reread,-- remains , if anything, even more "timely" than when it was written. For though we barely got through the retrospectively crazed Soviet-American nuclear face-off without blowing ourselves ---and the whole word --- up!, ----nowadays, thanks to the determination & ingenuity of <u>one</u> man, ( A.G. Khan, a PhD metallurgist from Pakistan who, these days, has become a kind of covert "populist" national hero in his own country, ) we *now* have another terrible quandary in front of us! ...Because of Khan's theft from the Dutch in 1974 (when he was working for Holland's national nuclear research agency) with access to the latest in centrifuge uranium enhancement technology, not only was Pakistan enabled to stay abreast of its deadly enemy, India, in the production of nuclear weapons, but Kahn himself subsequently turned into a kind of nuclear Santa Claus for megalomaniacs ,peddling his pilfered Pandora's box of secrets to his dear pals, (like Gaddafi in Libya ,and Kim Jong II in North Korea and others..) --------leaving all of us with a good chance of having to confront smuggled suitcase nukes some time in our futures!!

And then there's the surreal science fiction activities of our elite corps of ex-airborne fighter pilots, now grounded but currently maneuvering armadas of deadly remote controlled drones from their secret, code-named , hideaways, obliterating whatever human "targets" they're ordered to obliterate ,as easily as shooting fish in a barrel !..( Whilst simultaneously *ignoring,* of course, that constitutionally stipulated system of checks and balances we're *supposed* to be living under ----i.e. juries, judges, the rule of law, the presumption of innocence, the right to confront one's accusers, etc ------ all the stuff we were all taught to be so patriotically proud of in High School, where it was often piously invoked as some great treasure handed down to us by the wise Founding Fathers -------- guaranteed "built-in" bulwark of "justice" and equality for what was to become the world's most exemplary (&envied-from-afar) small d democratic Society – something underlined again by the giant paper mâché replica of the Statue of Liberty standing in New York Harbor, defiantly hosted aloft by angry protesters in Tiananmen Square in 1989, minutes before their wholesale slaughter began.

That's why "Journey South" seems, to me, more than ever, essential reading, and why I've become determined to see it into print, so that the unspeakable danger it illuminates, ----the incestuous spread of what has now become a hijacked, burst-open Pandora's box of a truly frightful technology ----rendered visible, for everyone with the courage and fortitude to stare at it------ (with it's cataclysmic potential)------ head-on! Indeed,- for all I know,-- some of you,-- after reading "Journey South" , -- may be tempted --or inspired--- to go out and start raising holy hell about this suicidal, and obviously deranged --state of affairs !... . If so, I urge you to make your *own* feelings known, not only for the future of *your kids* and *our* kids, --but of everybody *else's* kids' as well! ) --- In whatever ways -and *wherever* and *whenever*---- you can, A-men!

------Alan **Marcus** (Marcus Legacy Archives (#2)

*The last century was supposed to've improved upon previous*
*centuries But too many things, somehow, happened along the*
*way that weren't supposed to happen..*

*Winter and Spring, among other things*
*were supposed to be moving much closer together (Never*
*Happened!) Fear and Violence, it was said, , had been tracked*
*down to specific poverty stricken neighborhoods,*
*which were scheduled to be rendered peaceful*
*by specially trained emissaries, proficient with mandolins*

*Various ancient Scourges i.e. "Slavery,", "Hunger," "Warfare" Etc.*
*---were supposed to be gone from Radar screens.. Anybody still*
*seeing them, however, is invited to attend several forthcoming*
*Seminars on this subject: (For more info, please leave name &*
*address at the front desk ...)*

*Recognition of the helplessness of helpless ( i.e. jobless!) folk.. As*
*well as awareness (or its lack! )of their daily suffering..,*
*-is expected to be among High Priority items singled out for*
*Public Discussion...*
*After, -.that is,--- proof that the Gov's "official" Blockade of*
*smuggled-out photos of various friends, neighbors, colleagues ,*
*now sleeping-{& urinating} –in nearby parks, cars, alleyways,*
*garages ,closets, & public toilets,)--- has been called off !*
*Signatures to that effect are now being witnessed (we're told)*
*behind Closed Doors...*

*Even God himself (rumors say)*
*has begun taking a worried look at His*
*notoriously fratricidal (& bitterly lamented) earthly Creation*
*----in hopes of restoring whatever crucial items may have been*
*(disastrously! ) left out, during His famous (First) Appearance as*
*Front Man for the Miracle Biz...*

*"How should we live then?" somebody asked me the other day*
*(it was the same question I'd been waiting to ask him!)*

*All of which confirms, of course,*
*(as the above examples make clear)-*
*--- such questions of a similar Urgency*
*somehow end up (inexplicably!) coupled with the word "Naive"(!)*
*------to me, an astonishing fact , which, so far as I know, my*
*mentors are still, unable-or -(for reasons unknown,)---*
*unwilling to spell out why ....*

**Inspired by a poem of Wistaya** *Szymborska*
*(Polish Nobel Laureate in Literature---1996}*

# NOTE TO READER

For those who may be strange to movie parlance the following are some common expressions among movie making folk:

DISSOLVE = A lapse of time and/or space

O.S. = Out of Scene

V.O. = Voice Over

B.G.

F G.

In utter silence, on an empty screen, the following words:

*"ARE WE TO HAVE A CHANCE TO LIVE? WE DON'T ASK FOR PROSPERITY*

*OR EVEN SECURITY. ONLY FOR A REASONABLE CHANCE TO LIVE, TO*

*WORK OUT OUR DESTINY IN PEACE AND DECENCY ..."*

*- George Wald*
*Nobel Prize, Medicine- 1968*

# *PROLOGUE:*

A.      EXT. CAR WINDSHEILD, the face of a black cat. (Name: "Finney" - short for Finnegan). Staring at us from behind the glass of a moving car- steady, cryptic, aloof, expressionless, at night. We are in Arizona, in the desert country of the southwest. B.G. SOUND of humming motor, windshield wipers sweeping back and forth to clear away the night mist.

**CAR RADIO**
***All I Want***
*(rock and roll, hard rock)*

***Is a little bit of luuve...***
***All I need***
***Is a little bit of luuve ..."***

PULL BACK. Behind cat in the front seat are two people: a young man and older woman, The young man, RO (ROWAN) WILLIAMS , is 30; he is driving. He is a tall intelligent, weary, bony, ironic graduate student; lines of fatigue and intelligence mark his face. The woman, HELEN (MRS.) McALLISTER, is slumped down, looking out dreamily . She is in her late 30's or possibly 40. A very handsome, full-bodied woman, she wears a shawl against the desert chill.

**CAR RADIO**
**"All I ask**
**Is a little bit of luuve . ..**
**All I crave**
**Is a little bit of luuve..."**

B.      INT, CAB of huge six-ton truck . It is hurtling through the night. The DRIVER is in profile, a man in his mid- 50's, wearing a peaked cap, smoking a cigar.

**TRUCK RADIO**
**". ..suffering from a pulled groin muscle, is going to be out of action for at least two weeks, it was learned today ..."**

B.      *EXT. MOVING GREEN MUSTANG SEDAN, car in which the cat, Helen and Ro are riding, as it comes up to a line of cars and stops . Traffic jam- perhaps an accident ahead. A trunk road bears to the left.*

## CAR RADIO
*(organ music, saccharine)*
**"Friends: there is no better way to decorate for any festive occasion** ...

C.      *INT. MUSTANG as the driver, Ro, makes a sudden decision .
He pulls the car left and starts off, to avoid the logjam of cars ahead.*

## CAR RADIO
**...than with a Della Robia wreath from Boys Republic. Support
this free philanthropic tax exempt organization ..."**

E.      INT. TRUCK PANEL. We see a radio dial and a CLOCK . The
clock, a typical electric panel clock, shows 11:30 PM.

## TRUCK RADIO
**"...but a spokesman repeated emphatically: the only meetings in
Paris we know of are thEs ones held every week on Thursday.
Adam Rafael, CBS News, Paris.**"

F.      *INT. GREEN MUSTANG. As the cat suddenly leaps from the
windshield to the dozing woman's lap. She wakes up, bemused.*

## CAR RADIO
**"...casualty reports issued today by allied commands ,
reflects that the South Vietnamese forces ..."**

G.      *ON RO, as he turns on another trunk road, concentrating, rubbing
his eyes.*

## CAR RADIO
**"...are playing an increasing combat role.
Saigon forces lost 497 men killed in action...**"

H.      *ON TRUCK DRIVER, cigar, belly, peaked hat, he reaches a hand
out, absently scratches his chest.*

**"...what is the danger to America today? Are hippies the vanguard of a new revolution? This week I take ..."**

I.      WHEELS of the huge truck , rushing pell mell along a  two lane' highway.

**CAR RADIO**
**"...a long hard look at revolutions past and present..."**

J.      *CAR WHEELS of the green mustang, as they arrive at another crossroads and veer left again, south upon a desert road, two laned.*

**CAR RADIO**
**"...seven days a week  with plenty of free parking ..."**

K.      MOVING, FROM CAB of hurtling truck. A kaleidoscopic blur, the south western desert country .

**TRUCK RADIO**
*(sickly sweet violin music)*
**"...weekends are made for fun. This weekend why not take the whole family out to..."**

L.      *MOVING ROADWAY, hurtling under front wheels of mustang.*

M.      *She is now driving. As she reaches forward, twirls the radio dial to change the station, producing small interval of silence .*

**CAR RADIO**
**"...if I had million dollars I'd put up thousands of billboards: America , back to God! Get people God-conscious, America-conscious ..."**

N.      *ON RO AND CAT. Ro's face responds to the radio: an ironic sorrowful smile.*

**CAR RADIO**
**"...let's get rid of all those who are against us, against this country ..."**

TRUCK DRIVER. He is listening to his radio more attentively , perhaps even nodding his head in approving emphasis .

## TRUCK RADIO
**"...sad to say, friends , but America is being delivered over to re-pro-bate minds. They don't want God, they took the Bible out of schools...**

O.    *EXT. ANOTHER CROSSROADS as the huge truck comes up and turns left.*

P.    *Hesitates, and turns right.*

## CAR RADIO
**"...no, it seems they are protecting the criminal."**

Q.    ON RO dozing. Cat leaps back to its windshield perch. Helen, driving, peering straight ahead. Swirls of ground fog.

## CAR RADIO
**"May God have mercy on the innocent party...
...but friends , we are coming to that place.
Will the Lord come? Will He take me home?..."**

R.    *ON TRUCK DRIVER. As, with one hand, he fishes in his pocket, puts on glasses to see better. Ground fog very bad.*

## TRUCK RADIO
**"...will He take you home? Will the rapture take place?
But will you go to heaven empty-handed**? ..."

S.    EXT. WINDSHEILD mustang. The cat staring out at us.

## CAR RADIO
**"...6 million, 10 thousand shares, showing a downward trend, with losses mostly across the board..."**

T.    CLOSE: The dash of the truck, featuring the clock.
THE CLOCK SHOWS SIX MINUTES TO TWELVE !

## CAR RADIO
**"...71.3 kilocycles with the power of 5,000 watts under authority of the Federal Communications Commission. Until tomorrow at 7:30 AM ,thank you and good night.**
(Pause. Then the Star Spangled Banner starts in to play, loud, martial, a sign-off of this small southwestern station) .

U.    **EXT. A WOODEN BRIDGE**, narrow, and none to new,

spanning a swollen from the recent rains creek, perhaps a tributary of the Gila in Arizona. It is deserted. We can HEAR the distant approach of two not-so- distant engines, one heavier than the     other. Headlights appear from two directions, banding the ghostlike, darkened landscape. The motors get LOUDER very quickly.

V.      **WHEELS** of the speeding mustang. They suddenly turn violently, fiercely wrenched to one side, LOUD screech of brakes, wheels of the truck crossing the centerline, inexorably out of control. Star Spangled Banner playing LOUD.

W.      **INT. TRUCK DASHBOARD CLOCK**. A horrifying, stupefying off-stage CRASH. The clock glass shatters. The Star Spangled Banner continues to play. HOLD STEADY on this shattered clock.

### O.S. SOUND of a cat
-a loud single cry. FREEZE FRAME. BEGIN CREDITS, superimposed over the frozen and shattered clock.

# GEMINI

"SIGNS GOOD TODAY FOR TRAVEL,

TRY NEW VENTURES.

ASPECTS VERY FAVORABLE FOR

SUSTAINED MOMENTUM..."

1.      *EXT. COASTAL HIGHWAY - NORTHERN CALIFORNIA-
        MORNING.*

*MEDIUM CLOSE on Helen McAllister, bringing her car to a sudden halt to
tense SCREECH of the brakes. She's wearing sunglasses, is dressed in a
stylish suit, and has a vaguely professional air – a very attractive woman in
her 40's with one grown up daughter and a crusading Episcopalian Minister
of a husband, who is in a struggle with his well-heeled congregation, trying
to get them to realize that flinching from acknowledging the degrading life
stifling inequalities the US is presently inflicting upon one-third of its
population makes a mockery of the real meaning of the hymns they love to
sing each week during Sunday prayers. Meanwhile music form a portable
tape recorder nearby is playing the last movement of Beethoven's Sonata
Opus 31 in B Minor.*

2.      REVERSE ANGLE middle of the road. A neat line of small stones- a
        very modest "roadblock." Propped up by sticks behind is a large
        hand-lettered sign:


                    **PLEASE! TAKE THE SCENIC ROUTE!**

                         **(ARTIST AT WORK)**.

*CAMERA SLOWLY RISES to reveal a young man, very intent, peering
through a Polaroid camera viewfinder which is set up on a tripod pointing
toward a small telescope. The telescope itself wedged between two tree
branches, is focused upon an area shimmering in sunlight, hovering over
the middle of the highway, over which a large branch of a roadside oak
spreads its capillary tentacles.*

*At the sound of an objecting automobile horn. The young man looks up,
obviously diverted from his otherworldly concentration. He smiles a very
wide, open smile. His eyes are very deep. We are looking at Ro, of course.
CAMERA PANS he slowly away from tree, still holding his Polaroid with
tripod attached. He makes a gallant bow at Helen clearly as if to say: why
not drive around, lady?*

3.      ON HELEN. As she shakes her head: No, she points O.S.

4.      CLOSE UP Highway Department sign, in the sand off the graveled
        road: SOFT SHOULDER.

        *PULL BACK to Ro, smiling, unhurried, walks in to the shot. He is*

*standing near the sign. He stomps on the sand once or twice, then stops
and looks up, as if to say: see? No Problem. O.S. MUSIC still playing
LOUD.*

5.        *ON HELEN, shakes her head, another bemused refusal.*

**HELEN**
**Not that- excuse me, would you mind?**
*(She indicates the tape recorder. A beat, and the music is lowered)*
**Not that I'd ever want to stand in the way of an "artist".**
(ironic)
**Only I rather suspect they had something a little more weighty in
mind?**

6.        ON RO, as CAMERA SLOWLY PANS him from side of the road to
          Helen's car.

**RO**
**All they had in mind, sweet friend, was how to put a lot of
surplus sign painters to work.**
**Besides, the "artist" isn't me, I am just a disciple. Friend. Voyeur.**
*(he tears off a print from his camera, waves it once,
and gives it to het to look at)*
**This - if you happen to be interested - was what we were
working on, when you began leaning on your horn.**

7.        *CLOSE SHOT, the Polaroid print. It is a picture of a wondrous,
          fragile, but still unfinished giant spider web, the filaments reflect
          the light producing a wonderful prismatic effect, but the spider
          itself is not present.*

**RO (v.o.)**
**If we're patient, however. *And* lucky. *And* let Mr. Beethoven-
as the saying goes, do his thing. He might –
I emphasize the word *might*- reappear.**

8.        TWO SHOT Helen and Ro. She is looking at the photograph,
          she can't help admiring it. On the other hand, she wants to get
          the hell out of there.

**HELEN**
**Very lovely. But, look-**

**RO**
*(with complete ingenuousness)*
**Do you happen to know the poet, Hopkins? Gerald Manley Hopkins?**
*(he closes his eyes, concentrating)*
**There's a line of his...**
*(opening his eyes, recalling)*
**"*The whole earth testifies to the glory of God; it flows forth like Shining from -*"**
*(he stops, stuck again) .*


**HELEN**
*(smiling, finishing the line)*
**Shook *foil.*"**

*They look at each other, smile: there is a flash of implicit kinship born from the knowledge that both of them know this poem. Suddenly another horn abruptly intrudes.*

8.      RO AND HELEN'S P.O.V. A truck, halted before the roadblock, its driver acoustically objecting.

9.      *ON RO AND HELEN. He holds up his hand to the truck driver in pantomime, signaling wait a moment. He makes a gesture to Helen; will you permit me? She slides away from the driver's seat, letting him get in behind the wheel, rubs his hands together expertly, revs the motor, preparatory to making an expert assault on the soft shoulder.*


DISSOLVE:

---

10.     *CLOSE. A tire uselessly spinning , caught in the loose roadbed. O.S. SOUND of a motor laboring. It STOPS. SOUND of a door opening and closing.*

12.     *HELEN'S CAR, its left rear wheel stuck in the soft sand. As Ro leaves the driver's seat, retrieves a pole, motions to Helen with another hand.*

        *She comes into shot I.S, and settles herself behind the wheel, sighing, shaking her head.*

24

**RO (o.s.)**
**Okay.**

*She revs the motor up herself now.*
*The car buckles, but doesn't break free.*
*CAMERA CLOSES to Helen's face.*

**HELEN (v.o.)**
**There are times when I am afraid -**
**when a knowledge of Gerald Manley  Hopkins...**

13.     *ON RO. He is now using a larger pole to try to wedge the car*
*loose, straining against the back bumper as the wheel spins.*

**HELEN (v.o.)**
**...is less appealing than an elementary knowledge of the**
**fulcrum and lever!**

*The pole suddenly cracks in two! Ro is tumbled into the sand,*
*he sits there staring ruefully at the spinning wheel.*

DISSOLVE:

---

14.     MEDIUM HELEN, sitting on a stone wall, chin glumly in hand.
O.S. the continuing comic useless SOUND of the laboring car
motor.

**HELEN (o.s.)**
**Not that the time was entirely wasted, of course. For instance , I**
**learned - waiting interminably for the tow truck -**
*(she gets off the stone wall and begins to pace the highway, CAMERA*
*staying on her)*
**that a Gemini in Virgo - *me*- is definitely apt to be high**
**strung , impulsive, nervous-**
*(she turns on her heel and begins to walk back with a sigh)*
***and* impatient!**

15.     SHOWING RO, CAR, AND A FARMER WITH A HORSE. Ro is
attaching a rope to the front bumper with a bravura, confident
air.

**HELEN (v.o.)**
...while a Pisces in Libra -*him* -
is just as definitely apt to be...

*Ro gets into the car, starts the motor. The farmer beats the horse. The rope strains, the wheels churn.*

**HELEN (v.o.)**
...optimistic ,energetic ...

16.    *CLOSE SHOT front bumper, as the rope snaps in two.*

**HELEN (v.o.)**
...and *impracticable!*

DISSOLVE:

---

17.    *TWO SHOT Ro and Helen, strolling on the sand of nearby beach. Ro, talking earnestly, gently; Helen gravely listening.*

**HELEN (v.o.)**
I also learned - in case you're interested -that the ocean comprises
68 percent of the earth's surface - and is getting rather dirty.

18.    CLOSE SHOT FEET of Helen and Ro. He is barefoot.

**HELEN (v.o.)**
That most manufactured shoes are a premeditated crime...
(she removes her own shoes and is now barefoot)against the
metatarsal arch.

19.    *HELEN AND RO on a nearby boardwalk. She is eating a hamburger. He is eating grapes out of a brown paper bag. He refuses a bite of her hamburger - mock horror.*

**HELEN (v.o.)**
That eating meat - if you will pardon the expression -
according to the Chara Samitra of India -
dampens one's digestive fire.

20.     *HELEN, sitting on sand. Ro explaining what he is about to do, then*
*slowly, superbly, standing on his head in a classic position of meditation.*

### HELEN (v.o.)
**...also that Sisshamansa- among Yoga positions- can definitely**
**improve the functioning of the brain, the pineal gland, and the**
**pituitary gland - not to mention God knows how many other**
**indispensable organs!**

### DISSOLVE:

---

21.     *Another part of the beach. Ro and Helen. He has taken off his*
        *shirt. A magnificent specimen. He is ruffling with several of*
        *Helen's books. One is open. He is shaking his head sadly*
        *about it, talking to her earnestly.*

### HELEN (v.o.)
**Actually, he was very gentle with me,**
**considering what a mess he found me in.**
*(As Ro closes the book and pushes it away from him)*
**My books, for instance- comparative literature, emphasis on Latin-**
**American novelists- were "useless." They "degraded" things, you**
**see. Categorized them into mere "problems."**
**A national disease, etc.**

22.     *Ro, gently turning on his tape recorder, on a seagull on a rock,*
        *trying to catch the gul's sudden outburst of song.*

### HELEN (v.o.)
**His *own* work in progress, on the other hand - the one he**
**hadn't gotten around to writing yet, naturally-**

23.     *Helen, seated on the sand, chin in hands, enchanted*
        *watching this spiritual enthusiast.*

### HELEN (v.o.)
**...was going to be made up entirely of sounds recorded on his**
**travels** ...

24.     *MOVING - Helen and Ro. He is enthusiastically pointing out to*
        *her things O.S.*

**HELEN (v.o.)**
**...full of the spontaneity of actual life, the hidden meanings of**
**"found" objects**...

*They stop walking, and Ro poses Helen against a backdrop of*
*cypresses, backs away O.S. to take her picture, CAMERA*
*centering on her.*

**HELEN (v.o.)**
**Like me for instances. I was a "found object."**

25.     CLOSE- driftwood on the beach accompanied by
        O.S. CLICK of camera.

**HELEN (v.o.)**
**...ditto for driftwood** ...

25.     CLOSE - several bottles, aged by the sea,
        posed on a ledge of rock .

**HELEN (v.o.)**
**...beach glass**...

26.     *Group of children playing jump rope on the sand, chanting .*

**HELEN (v.o.)**
**...children's voices...**

27.     *Helen and Ro walking together, she has her arm now through*
        *his; he still lecturing gently, but gravely.*

**HELEN (v.o.)**
**...and all those other reverberating miracles which- if I only**
**made the effort -I could decipher myself, at will.**

28.     *EXT. COASTAL ROAD as the car is being pulled out of the ditch*
        *by a tow truck, while Helen and Ro watch.*

#### HELEN (v.o.)
**As a student , however, I was distinctly _un_promising ...**

CAMERA MOVES FORWARD losing Ro and Helen, concentrating on car.

#### HELEN (v.o.)
**Defending that 300 horsepower smog machine, which I absolutely refused to abandon in a ditch...?**

29.     ANOTHER ANGLE featuring Helen and Ro and the excavated car. As Helen gathers up her things and walks toward the driver's seat.

#### HELEN (v.o.)
**...Cherishing the memory of dead poets whose words I refused to live by...!**
*(she is now inside her car, getting ready to drive off)*

**30.**  Con:
     **...sleeping on a box spring and mattress, which- horrors- did all sorts of unspeakable things to my spine!**

DISSOLVE:

---

31.     MOVING- Helen in her car, driving along a coastal road.

#### HELEN (v.o.)
**Obviously, I am an artifact! Sort of a one woman chamber of  horrors of the Obsolete Generation...**

*CAMERA PULLS BACK, loses Helen, to reveal Ro on a bicycle, hooking a ride along the highway, holding on to Helen's car. He is giving himself to the beautiful scenery, taking several deliberate salutary deep breaths.*

#### HELEN (v.o.)
**...while _him,_ with his relentless breathing exercises...**

CAMERA MOVES to show Ro's equipment on the back of the bicycle - telescope, tape recorder, camera, etc..

**HELEN (v.o.)**
*(continuing)*
**...poetry dousing equipment - smokeless transportation...**

32.　Beautiful old redwood tree near the entrance to a college campus. A vegetable patch spreads around it, carefully tended, there is a rope ladder hanging down and distinctly visible in F.G.

**HELEN (v.o.)**
**...not to mention a brand new
made-it-myself tree house!**

33.　*TWO SHOT Helen and Ro, standing amidst the blooming vegetable patch. He is picking some fresh vegetables for her; she looks at him, she sighs, she is enchanted in spite of herself. He expression would be quizzical, if she weren't - somewhere deep inside of her - sensually stirred.*

**HELEN (v.o.)**
**...my God, I was obviously in touch with the future itself!**

*Ro throws her a tomato, she catches it. He walks over to her; their eyes catch. She takes a slow deliberate bite; they do not cease looking at one another. She continues to eat the tomato .*

**HELEN (o.s.)**
**...and everybody knows how hard it is for the Future and the Past, as they say, to com-mun-i-cate  nowadays -don't we?**

DISSOLVE:

---

34.　EXT. TREEHOUSE LADDER - AFTERNOON.

SLOW PAN. (NOTE: During this subsequent scene, until the time indicated - the CAMERA will SLOWLY PAN up the rope ladder to the entrance of the treehouse, and then begin a SECOND PAN along the walls of the treehouse inself, at a specific time which will also be indicated).

## PRESIDENT NIXON'S VOICE (v.o. on tape)
What's your name, solder?

## SOLDIER (v.o.)
Jones, Mr. President. Specialist Fourth Class, Leroy Jones.
Poughkeepsie, New York?

## NIXON'S VOICE (v.o.)
Tell me, Leroy, you prefer the Mets or the Yankees?

## SOLDIER (v.o.)
I'll stick with the Yankees, sir...

## NIXON'S VOICE (v.o.)
They always stick with the winning team, don't they? Well, you
could be wrong this year, Leroy, we'll just have to see and wait.
Right fellas?

## PHOTOGRAPHER (v.o.)
Mr. President, could we have a shot of you shaking hands
over to the left a little?

35.  INT. TREEHOUSE. SLOW PAN. We see the walls of a very
eclectic austere bachelor's hideaway. Tacked to the plywood wall are a
series of blown up photographs; of young people who have burned or
hurt themselves in protest against the conditions of the world they live in
(Morrison, the Quaker who burned himself up in front of the U.N.; Jan
Palmach, the Czech who burned himself up in protest against the
Russian invasion of Czechoslovakia; various Vietnamese Buddhist nuns
and monks, etc.). Above each photograph of the immolated suicide is
the name and date of the vent, neatly printed and visible. Interposed
between each of these photographs are a series of blown up and
horrible Vietnamese atrocities, both north and south. The crescendo of
this SLOW PAN will end with a blown up picture of President Nixon's
visit to Di Nam in the summer of 1969, surrounded by a crush of
correspondents. One of them, in dark glasses, tall very young, arms
frantically outstretched to catch the President's remarks on a portable
tape recorder, is obviously a younger version of Ro. This image of Ro is
encircled in a rough red crayon.

## NIXON'S VOICE (v.o.)
How about this big fella with a handle bar mustache?

SOLDER (v.o.)
(shouting out in a triggered response)
Petronelli, sir! Corporal James! Nashville, Tennessee!

NIXON'S VOICE (v.o.)
How's the chow, Corporal? Any complaints?

AD LIB SOLDIERS (v.o.)
No complaints, Mr. President...
It's okay...
We're doin' all right, sir...

SLOW PAN. (NOTE: During this subsequent scene, until the time indicated - the CAMERA will SLOWLY PAN up the rope ladder to the entrance of the treehouse, and then begin a SECOND PAN along the walls of the treehouse, at a specific time which will also be indicated).

NIXON'S VOICE
"Always gives me a terrific lift when I get a chance to get out in the field, meet some of you fellas in the flesh. As I said before - and I want to make it perfectly clear- in my judgment we've never fielded a more intelligent or gutsy group in our country's history. And I'd say that a nation that can do that, and at the same time be the first country in the world to put men on the surface of the moon, just simply has got to have a lot, as you fellas say-goin' for it- am I right?"


"Right...
Yes, sir!"

AD LIB SOLDIERS (o.s.)
We're with you, Mr. President~!"...

36.     TWO SHOT RO AND HELEN. They are lying together, naked under a sheet, on a straw mat. Helen is smoking, chin propped up, listening intently to Ro, who has just shut off a small tape recorder in one hand.

RO
"It wasn't only that small town baseball chatter- it was his look!" That same lunatic look you used to see on the faces of all those uniformed cheerleaders. Leaping over their desks with their

32

**goddam blackboard pointers to show you the weekly crop of alphabetic atrocities - FKRs, Friendly Kill Ratios, FIAs, Friendly Initiated Actions, etc.-**

37.     CAMERA CLOSES IN on Ro, momentarily losing Helen.

**RO**
(continuing)
**"I became scared of one day *not being* scared. I mean, of needing to get high on bullets, like everybody else. Turning into a sort of spiritual "TC" - another gorgeous phrase! TC - *"Tolerable casualty!"***
(he smiles. A change of tone, jokingly)
**Try it-you'll find it has a sort of soothing ring.** (in a mocked chant)
**"I'm a tolerable casualty! You're a tolerable casualty! He's a tolerable casualty!"**

38.     ON HELEN. Draped in a sheet, the last picture on the wall in her hand- the one of Ro as correspondent. As she turns back to the straw mat, CAMERA PANS her back to a TWO SHOT with Ro.

**HELEN**
(*quizzically following his lead*)

**"he's a tolerable casualty, she's a tolerable casualty, we're *all* tolerable casualties.!"..**

*She is now back beside him, reclining. She studies the photograph in her hands.*

39.     CLOSE SHOT the photograph, as earlier described.

**HELEN (o.s.)**
**"You were fatter. Right?"**

**RO (o.s.)**
**I was eating more, let's say. But enjoying it less.**

**HELEN (o.s.)**
**"My God, I can feel the man's rib cage! How about that?"**

**RO (o.s.)**
**Ditto.**

40.     TWO SHOT RO AND HELEN.

HELEN

That's what I call mag-na-ni-mi-ty.

RO

All right, five minutes. Don't worry , I'll locate it-

HELEN
(*waving her finger, mock disapproval*)
Uh, uh. Not nice, not nice...
(*lighter tone*)
You're not supposed to remind me that I'm a-----what's that
expression -"tolerable casualty?"
(*an attempt at insouciance*)
Besides, since we've both played this scene before? Dozens
of times? On the late late show?

RO
Uh uh.
(*contradicting*)

(*detailed reasons*)
One: no motorcycle! Two: I also lack a scowl. For the poh-lice.
Have to have a scowl for the poh-lice.

HELEN
And I have to get furious,  of course.

RO
Why?

HELEN
Because you stared, you brute! I mean, I'm an old hag and you're a
young man. And you stared. Afterwards! Cru-el!

RO
(*swinging into parody, with enthusiasm*)
How could I help it? You're beautiful!

40. Cont.

HELEN
(*ironic*)
Ravishing!

                         **RO**
                       You are.

                       **HELEN**
                        **Sure.**
                   (*the irony caricatured*)

                         **RO**
                      **I mean it.**

                       **HELEN**
                       **Uh huh.**
                         **RO**
                  (*hands under his neck,
           eyes at the ceiling, composing his "lines"*)
                     **Come here.**

                       **HELEN**
              **No. Translation- hurry up!**
                   (*a pause. She is stuck*)
                     **Now what?**

                         **RO**
        **Hey, how about I remind you of your son?**
        **Who would have been my age. Had he lived.**

                       **HELEN**
   **And you *could* keep assuring me how much groovier it is**
                 **with an older woman right?**
                   (*shakes her head*)
   **No, wait. Strike that! Let's just cut to the anatomy lesson.**
        **You know, entwined bodies. White on white.**

41.    *CLOSE ON HELEN'S FINGERS. As they were only a few
       minutes earlier in the fever on lovemaking, clutching at Ro's
       shoulder.*

                       **RO (o.s.)**
              **Digging into his shoulders** ...

41.    CLOSE ON HELEN'S NAKED BREASTS crushed against Ro.

**HELEN (o.s.)**
Her breasts?

**RO (o.s.)**
They swell.

42.     CLOSE HELEN'S PROFILE . At the acme of lovemaking, damp
and thrown back.

**HELEN (o.s.)**
Face?

**RO (o.s.)**
Sweaty.

CAMERA MOVES IN concentrating on Helen's eyes, tightly shut.

**HELEN (o.s.)**
Eyes?

**RO (o.s.)**
Zonked.

**HELEN (o.s.)**
Sound effects? Waves?

43.     The two of them lying there as they were before, staring at the
ceiling, side by side, alternately improvising "lines."

**RO**
Come on! This is the 1970's, buster! Stick to where to action is.

**HELEN**
At one point she cries out his name?

44.  Cont.

**RO**
(*in mock disgust*)
How could she, they just met, right?
(*a sort of mock passionate summing up*)
Besides, names don't matter, age doesn't matter! It's *souls* that
matter! They're fellow graduate students, that's all.

The hell with biography!
(*descriptive, matter of fact*)
She's a groovy grandma, she commutes three times a week.
He claims to be some kind of health nut, lives up in a tree.


HELEN

(giving him a sudden look, breaking the "scene")
You never saw anything like that on the late late show!

*She suddenly darts O.S., carrying part of a blanket draped around her.*
*Ro sits up cross-legged, half covered by a sheet, talking toward her O.S.*

HELEN

Funny. The most erotic scenes in movies have nothing to do with
the eye. Remember "Persona?" The nurse *telling* the actress - or
was it the other way around?- how she seduced that young boy, I
think ,on the beach? "He struck and struck again!" Or "*Weekend*?"
Sitting there on a table in her slip telling of that triangular orgy...

45.     MOVING, ON Helen, as she wanders around the room,
        inspecting, blanket trailing after her like a Bedouin.
        She picks up a shirt, looks at it, and shakes her head.

HELEN
Where're your sewing things?
(*she pulls open a drawer*)
You've only got one button left on-
(*stops. Sees what's in a drawer*)
Oh, goodie, hats!
(*reaches into a drawer and puts on a large child's space helmet,*
*her voice immediately assumes the boy scout*
*eloquence of the space explorers*)
"Tremendous sight, Houston.
Colors are really really tremendous. Over."

RO (o.s.)
"You're looking real good, Valley Forge.
Right on the button. Over."

HELEN
"Real fine Houston. Right now we can see old terra firma off
the left porthole, the view is really really great. The earth looks
sort of like a great big shiny round...
(*groping*)
...ball."

37

*(she takes off the space helmet, rummages around in the drawer, sticks on a Russian fur cap)*
"Horoshoh, Tovarish. *Really Horoshoh.*"

### RO (o.s.)
Translation: Real real great.

*PAN as Helen leaves bureau, inspects bookcase, kneeling down, blanket still trailing like a Bedouin.*
### HELEN
And look, my God, books. The man reads!

*(quoting from a book she has slipped out of the shelves)*
"...you can recognize truth by its beauty and simplicity ... easy when you have made a guess and done two or three calculations ,to make sure it's not obviously wrong .To know it's right..."
*(she closes the book)*
**Which two** or three calculations?

### RO (o.s.)
Depends on what're you're trying to guess!
In his case- he's a physicist- some inkling of how long the universe may last. (If it lasts!) Question mark!

### HELEN
*(posturing)*
In **my** case, the future! The same *thing* - right?

45. **Helen** *moves back to bureau. CAMERA PANNING her, staying on her; while she rummages around. She pulls out and sticks on her head an imitation turban. Precariously balancing both turban and blanket, she goes toward Ro, spontaneously kneels; both are now IN CAMERA.*

### HELEN
Tell me, oh treehouse sage! The cards!
The fates! Etcetera! What do the stars foretell in my case?

### RO
In your case, Madam, we'll require a little more research!

*She leans forward, to a kiss. Ro suddenly pulls back in mock objection.*

**RO**
Wait! We're bolloxing everything again.
(*in a clipped explanation*)
You've had time to "reflect" - right? Your husband! My family!
The future! I mean, if I want a- forgive me- second round-
It seems I may have to force you.


**HELEN**
(*embracing him as the blanket slips off*)
Force me.

DISSOLVE:

---

46.     *INT. UNIVERSITY CLASSROOM.*

MEDIUM CLOSE on Helen. She is taking notes. She stops, and looks
up dreamily.


**HELEN (o.s.)**
(*her voice is slightly distorted, she is breathing very hard,
slowly coming down from a high point of lovemaking*)
I'm sorry. I really didn't mean-


**RO (o.s.)**
Forget it. *"No importa"*.


**HELEN (o.s.)**
Don't you have bandaids? I mean, really, I'm not in the habit of...

*Helen suddenly grabs her books up from her desk, walks out of her
classroom .*

47.     *EXT. CAMPUS as Helen emerges from the building, strolling on
the compound. Students around her. She is still lost, in a kind of
recollective reverie. The ANGLE is RATHER CLOSE.*


**RO (o.s.)**
Look, think of it as a trophy.
(*in mock bravado*)
"The poor old thing got so carried away
she took a chunk out of me!"

48.     INT. LIBRARY CUBICLE. Helen, trying to study, doodling space
        helmets on a piece of paper. She looks up, still impaled on her
        recent sexual epiphany .

**RO (o.s.)**
**Can't you picture it? Don Juan, swaggering in the locker room-?**
**Ow!**
(his tone changes to a yelp of pain)

**HELEN (o.s.)**
**Be my guest! Since you're shopping around for "trophies!"**

49.     *EXT. LIBRARY ENTRANCE as Helen comes out, books under*
        *her arm. She suddenly starts, and stares O.S.*

50.     MOVING- Ro on bicycle, gently riding across the commons.
        He doesn't see her.

**RO (o.s.)**
**Cannibal!** ...

**HELEN (o.s.)**
**Beast!...**

**RO (o.s.)**
**Vampire! ...**

51.     Helen, following with her eyes.

**HELEN (o.s.)**
(*a very sensual tone, a distinct softening*)
**Kiss me...**

DISSOLVE:

---

52.     ON HELEN in a cue of students, signing a petition: there is a
        table, tacked up posters, the usual paraphernalia of a student
        protest movement.

## RO (o.s.)
*(in B.G. one can HEAR Helen's still passionate breathing, plus a certain note of concentration on Ro's voice)*
**The atomic weight of iron is 55.8...**


## HELEN (o.s.)
**What's the matter?**


## RO (o.s.)
Shhh. Don't move.
*(resuming his determined count)*
**The atomic weight of cobalt is 58 point-**


## HELEN (o.s.)
**But you didn't!... I mean, I can still feel you're not-?**


53.    *ON RO. He is pushing a little cart into the quadrangle loaded with vegetables , inviting students to come and take their pick, free . Grinning, barefoot, jeans and T-shirt.*


## RO (o.s.)
**Kundalini. A branch of the Haga Yoga ...**


## HELEN (o.s.)
**Kunda - *what?***


## RO (o.s.)
**You can prolong everything indefinitely.
Only it requires a great deal of control.**
*(resuming his litany)*
**The atomic weight of copper is 63 point-**


54.    *ANOTHER ANGLE as Helen enters near the pushcart;
Ro sees her, smiles, makes a motion with his hand- take your pick.*


## HELEN (o.s.)
**The hell with Kundalini!**


## RO (o.s.)
**Quit that! You'll sabotage me, you bitch!**
## HELEN (o.s.)
**Amen!**

**RO (o.s.)**
Oh...


**HELEN (o.s.)**
*(as Ro rummages around, hands her a large, leafy carrot plant;*
*the plant which touches his hand, of course, touches hers;*
*they look at one another)*
**That's it! Ah, that's my treehouse boy. Oh, he's a love, isn't he?**
**Oh, he really and truly is!**

DISSOLVE:

------------------------

55.      EXT. NEARBY BEACH

56.      H. CLOSEUP a coral shell. This image is accompanied by a
CLICK, as of a camera taking a shot, and the subsequent images in this
sequence are all accompanied by a similar CLICK.

**RO (o.s.)**
**According to Simon Weil – who no doubt you never heard of-**


**HELEN (o.s.)**
**Snob!**

57.      CLOSE.A piece of driftwood, composed, framed by the sand.

**RO (o.s.)**
**"A truth is always a truth with reference to *something* ...**

57.      MEDIUM CLOSE.A cormorant, seated, riding on the water near
shore.

**HELEN (o.s.)**
**What's the big hurry? I mean, why don't we**
**get our feet wet, or something?**


**RO (o.s.)**
**She also said: "To desire truth, is to desire contact-"**

58.      BEACH. We see two pairs of bare feet moving, belonging to Ro
and Helen. LOSE RO as he goes forward out of sight, Helen stops.

42

**"-with a *radiant* piece of reality."**

*Clothes begin to fall at Helen's feet; a dress, a slip; obviously she is shedding right there on the sand spontaneously, on impulse.*

## RO (o.s.)
**"Particularized** ..."

A brassiere falls on top of the pile, and the CAMERA BEGINS TO RISE SLOWLY.

## RO (o.s.)
**Concrete ..."**

58. Cont.    Now the CAMERA has risen to disclose all of Helen's face, lovely, tremulous, and entreating.

## RO (o.s.)
**"...and *inimitable*..."**

## HELEN
*(saucy)*
**What's the matter, aren't I" inimitable" enough?**

*She holds out her hands; Ro comes from O.S. into the scene, into her arms.*

## DISSOLVE:

---

59.    EXT. TREE HOUSE SITE. Ro's garden. He is working, weeding, but with a book in one hand a hoe in the other. Stripped to the waist.

## HELEN (o.s.)
**"Ay que trabajo me questez come te quieno. Por tu amor me duelo el aire, el cerazor,, y el sombrero ..."**

60.    *HELEN, seated in the grass nearby, books spread out, studying, absorbed in the text; what she is reading is a poem by Garcia Lorca.*

*"How hard, ah how hard, To love you like this ...*

*For love of you, my dear The very air*

*my razor,*

*Even my silly hat itself,*

*Hurts..."*

### HELEN
(*takes off her hat, closes he eyes, calls O.S.*)
**Hey! C'mere! I want to read you something** ...
(*pause. After a few seconds Ro comes I.S.,
but he is absorbed in his own book.*)

### RO
(*referring to his own text*)
**"In the present war, no means is considered improper for
defeating the enemy ."**

(*challenging Helen*)
**Who said that? Name and year?**

### HELEN
(*as she closes her own book, and defers her own contribution*)
**Christian Dior?**
(*reflecting*)
**Oh no, wait. How about John Wayne!
Correction:** *Colonel* **John Wayne!**

### RO (o.s.)
**That's Ghandi ,friend. Deploring total war - 1916 style!**

### DISSOLVE:

---

61.     *HELEN AND RO moving on the parking lot toward Helen's car -
late afternoon. Ro is still quoting to her from his book.*

### RO
**"What am I to advise a man who wants to kill,
but is unable, owing to his being maimed?"**

44

CAMERA MOVES IN centering on Helen, losing Ro. For a second ,
unaware, she allows her enchantment with him -for a variety of reasons-
to show.

### RO (o.s.)
**"Before I can make him feel the virtue of *not* killing,
I must restore to him the arm he has lost..."**

62.    *ANOTHER ANGLE- the two of them. As she holds out her arms
to him, smiling.*

### HELEN
**Restore me to the car you once almost lost for me, Mahatma.
The hour groweth late...**

*Ro bends over, boldly catches her, lifts her up in his arms, and starts
walking to her car.*
62.  Cont.

### HELEN
(*continuing*)
**I c*ould* stay over? Call up, say I have to work late or something?**

### RO
**Uh uh.**
(*matter of fact*)
**Number one, I haven't cracked a book in four days. Number
two, you'll disturb a tricky experiment I've got planned.**

### HELEN
**Experiment?**
(*grinning*)

### RO
**You don't think I intend to give up Kundalini,
just because you won't cooperate?**

*He deposits her in a car, kisses her goodbye, and withdraws O.S.
CAMERA HOLDS on Helen, staring after him.*

### DISSOLVE:

---

63.   INT. HELEN'S CAR- MOVING- DUSK. She is driving along, replaying fragments of the afternoon, as it were, in her mind.

**HELEN (v.o.)**
**Ay que trabajo me cuesta queréte como te quiero ...**

64.   HELEN, seen through the glass of a public phone booth on a roadside filling station. She is in the middle of a telephone call; we can see her hands gesticulating.

**HELEN (o.s.)**
*Por tu amor me duele el aire el cerazor, el sombrero ...*

65.   ON Helen, at the wheel of her car, driving down the highway on the direction from which she had just come-in other words, *back* towards the University. Her expression has changed, alight with anticipation ; in fact, she rehearses in her mind the kind of dialogue that she hopes that in all likelihood may soon take place

65. Cont.

**HELEN (o.s.)**
**Item one: beds! I am becoming distinctly allergic. Give me plain boards any time. Progress?**

**RO (o.s.)**
**Encouraging.**

**HELEN (o.s.)**
**Item two: diet. Yin over yang, goodbye sweet tooth! Good?**

**RO (o.s.)**
**Very good!**

66.   *PARKING LOT, which is located some distance away from the treehouse, on campus, as Helen pulls in, and stops, and gets out of the car.*

**HELEN (o.s.)**
**Item three: The half-lotus. Look! Correction - make that almost the *three-quarters* lotus!**

46

**RO (o.s.)**
Congratulations! .

**HELEN (o.s.)**
Item four: portents. Neptune worries me. What do you advise?

67.    *RO'S VEGETABLE GARDEN- DUSK. Showing Helen slowly*
*threading her way through it toward the treehouse ladder,*
*expectant.*

**RO (o.s.)**
Neptune's definitely in a bad conjunction, Madam.
If I were you I'd stay home all week .

**HELEN (o.s.)**
In spite of the " Cinderella" syndrome?

**RO (o.s.)**
Cinderella?

67. Cont.

**HELEN (o.s.)**
There's this lady I know, doctor. She counts on turning
into Cinderella at least three times a week .

*Helen has now reached the ladder and begins slowly to climb up,*
*CAMERA HOLDING AND MOVING with her all the way. No sign of any*
*else about.*

**RO (o.s.)**
She needs help. Obviously Cinderella was nothing but a basket
case. Psychogenically speaking.

**HELEN (o.s.)**    *e*
How about Prince Charming than?

**RO (o.s.)**
A fiction. No such animal! Invention of a lot of female shut-ins.

**HELEN (o.s.)**
(*as she reaches the entrance to the treehouse itself*)
But he lived Happily Ever After?

68.     REVERSE ANGLE . What Helen sees: the treehouse is empty!

**RO (o.s.)**
**My dear Cinderella: nobody - and you have my exclusive**
**permission to quote me on this , too -lives Happily Ever After !**
**Exclamation point!**

DISSOLVE:

---

69.     *THE TREEHOUSE- NIGHT. On Helen. She has just finished*
*giving the place a thorough cleaning, setting it to rights,*
*propping up pillows, etc. She picks up a placard that has fallen*
*from a shelf, newly painted: "Green Power, Hallelujah!" She*
*smiles and props it up. She turns and walks back - nothing else*
*to do - where the ladder is.*

70.     *EXT. LADDER- TREEHOUSE- NIGHT, as Helen slowly,*
*dreamily, descends ladder, begins to walk CAMERA HOLDING*
*ON HER through the vegetable patch in the moonlight. She*
*suddenly reacts, as the SOUND O.S. of a car pulls up and stops. She*
*shrinks back a little, half in shadow, and stares O.S. We HEAR a car*
*door open and close, intermingled voices, O.S.*

71.     *REVERSE RATHER LONG ANGLE: What Helen sees: Ro and*
*a tall, dark, very attractive young woman his own age; they*
*stand by the parked car. Obviously, she's telling him something,*
*we can't hear what. He suddenly takes her in his arms.*

72.     *ON HELEN, she shrinks back into the shadows, desperately*
*quiet, melting away from the scene.*

DISSOLVE:

---

73.     INT. BEDROOM of HELEN AND HER HUSBAND'S
ELEGANTLY APPOINTED  TOWNHOUSE. MEDIUM CLOSE...

**INTERCOM**
**The time is 7.31 AM. Temperature is 63 degrees. Weather report,**
**cloudy turning to light drizzle later this afternoon. Chance of rain**
**20 percent today, 30 percent tomorrow.**

*A hand comes into scene, lifts the phone off the hook, hangs it up.*
*CAMERA PULLS BACK: we see a pair of woman's legs swing down*
*over the double bed, right now half occupied, and scrunch into a pair of*
*slippers.*

74.　　INT. BREAKFAST ROOM HELEN'S HOUSE.
　　　　　Showing one-half of a two place setting, the plate untouched.
　　　　　On wall in B.G. is an intercom.

### INTERCOM
**"...the Bishop called twice, three or four reporters.**
**There's a message from your husband too: he'll be at the airport,**
**Gate 31, twelve o'clock. Also, the garage won't have your car 'til**
**Friday –I don't know why -I can't understand the name of all those**
**parts... oh, and the back bathroom's stopped up again, we need a**
**new whatchamacallit- the thing that bobs**
**up and down in the tank."**

75.　　MEDIUM CLOSE Helen's feet, now shod in street shoes,
　　　　　placed beneath breakfast table. They suddenly move, walk to
　　　　　the wall: CLICK, intercom is switched off.

76.　　EXT. CITY SIDEWALK- MOVING, on Helen's feet. (NOTE:
　　　　　During this sequence, she will proceed along the sidewalk,
　　　　　cross a traffic boulevard and finally enter a large institutional
　　　　　building-the "sounds" will have to be spaced, obviously, to
　　　　　coincide with the length of the sequence.)

### LOUDSPEAKER FROM RECORD SHOP
*(blasting a rock and roll song)*
*"Back field in motion, baby*
*"You tried to pull a fast one on me Back field in motion, baby*
*Please don't make a move I can't see."*

### AUCTION LOUDSPEAKER
**"...Come on, ladies! Seventy-five dollars for this fantastic bargain?**
**This guaranteed gen-yoo-ine- please don't crowd up from, Miss-**
**there's plenty of room..."**

### (V.O.)
### SIDEWALK FORTUNETELLER
**"...Length of the little finger shows extreme flexibility, plus a**
**capacity to improvise. Perhaps the Native likes to consider several**
**possibilities at once, finally makes up her mind. Fate line and head**

line strongly conjoined; once the Native *does* make up her mind she has a habit of following through,-"

## POLICE DEPARTMENT RECORDING
*(at intersection- against a huge B.G. of traffic NOISES, horns, etc.)*
"...Cross upon yellow signal and between white lines only. Your cooperation is solicited; violators will be prosecuted.
*(pause)*
Cross upon yellow signal and between white lines only.
Your cooperation is solicited ..."

77.     INT. INSTITUTION ELEVATOR- GROUP SHOT, a covey of legs, most are white clad. Helen's prominent in F.G. Whining SOUND of elevator ascending.

77.  Cont.

## ELEVATOR RECORDING
*(introduced by a BELL TONE)*
"...second floor. Surgery. X-Rays. Geriatrics. Radio Biology.
Visitors register at room two-one-three.
Repeat- visitors must register at room two-one-three ..."

78.     INT. HOSPITAL WARD, on OLD LADY. MEDIUM CLOSE. Perhaps a charity patient; grizzled, dried up, toothless.

## OLD LADY
*(dictating to Helen nearby)*
President of the United States, White House, Washington, D.C.
Dear Dick...
*(another tone, looking up)*
Excuse me, dearie, will you pass me my teeth?
I can talk better with my teeth in.

She is handed her teeth. She puts them in, settles herself, getting ready to let fly.
*(continuing)*
Dear Dick...
*(to Helen O.S.)*
## OLD LADY
You tell me if I go too fast, Mrs. McAllister.
*(back on target)*
Dear Dick... the weather up here is fine, how is the weather down there? ...Well, at last I got one of those nice grey ladies to take down a letter as the nurses are so spiteful in this hospital and mean they won't even bring me the bedpan when I need it, in fact,

50

the whole service is just plain putrid!
(*to Helen*)
**P-u-t-r-i-d! Putrid!**

DISSOLVE:

---

INT. TAXICAB- MOVING- on DRIVER talking over his shoulder.

## DRIVER
I *know* it was the same guy knocked off **those** other cabbies,
but the police just sit there and smile:
(*he holds a finger of one hand at his head,
as if it were a pistol, in mimicry*)
"...bang, you're dead! ...bang, you're dead!" And then that real, like-
from-nutsville laugh!
(*a plaint*)
**Naturally, my wife wants me to quit.
But at my age, what else could I do?**

DISSOLVE:

---

79.    *INT. AIRPORT RAMP. On FATHER NICHOLAS McALLISTER,
aged 45; very handsome, though at the moment a ravaged
looking utterly fatigued. He is hands a slip of paper to Helen.*

## NICHOLAS
(*as he hands the paper to Helen, O.S.*)
**They don't like to break silence- that's the kind of Retreat it is.
But there's the number, just in case...**

(*he breaks off, as if his mind had wandered ,then snaps back*)

**...if I were you, I wouldn't even answer the phone right now. Get out
of the house. Go down to Las Fuentes awhile... I might even be
able to join you there afterwards--- that is, when I'm better able to
come to terms with-**

## (O.S.)
## AIRPORT  LOUDSPEAKER
**Father McAllister? Nicholas McAllister? Report Gate 31, flight**

seven-seven-three. Last call! Passengers westbound. Flight seven-seven-three. Eureka Airlines. Ready for immediate departure! Thank you.

### NICHOLAS
(leaning into CAMERA, under difficult control)
**Goodbye, my dear.**

### DISSOLVE:

---

80.    *INT. BACHELOR GIRL'S APARTMENT- NEW YORK CITY- on a young woman- very young, about 19 or 20- CAROL, Helen's daughter. She is dressed in bra and panties only, and is talking on the telephone. An air stewardess' cap perches, incongruous, on her head.*

### CAROL
**I can't hear very well, Mother- ...Retreat? ...*What* retreat? ...Look, maybe you better write, I mean, telephones are really, like, nowhere... She looks up and makes a mock gesture of slitting her throat to someone O.S.**

81.    *REVERSE ANGLE. BED. Avery handsome JAPANESE is reclining there, obviously naked under a sheet, smoking -the gesture was meant for him. He gestures with his hand to her: hurry up!*

### CAROL (o.s.)
**One of *my* flights? Beautiful!**

*The Japanese man starts to walk toward Carol, CAMERA PANNING HIM, he is in focus from the waist up. He is obviously nude.*

(continuing)
### CAROL
**Only look! Why don't you wait till I get transferred to a more civilized run, Mother? ...I mean, frankly, I don't think you'd *like* the Orient. As an attraction, it's really over-rated...**

*By now the Japanese man has come INTO CAMERA with Carol, and is caressing her, delicately undoing her bra, his face buried in her shoulder.*

(continuing)

52

### CAROL
You, too. Honest. Long letter. Tomorrow.

### DISSOLVE:

---

82.  *INT. DOCTOR'S OFFICE centering on a bald headed, exasperated , middle-aged GYNECOLOGIST. He slams a folder down on his desk and jumps from his chair, talking to Helen O.S.*

### GYNECOLOGIST
I don't care what Simone de Beauvoir or Lady Godiva or any other *female* authority says! You are not - repeat- *not*- in my highly considered opinion, going through any premature change, or anything like it. Period!
*(he sits down in a chair, little cooler)*

83.  Cont.
Please! Do me a favor! Go out and sit in a sauna! Get your hair done! Whatever it is you ladies do to finagle you out of these pre-menstrual flips. Let *me* tend to patients who are *really* sick. Okay?

*He smiles and comes forward to shake her hand- an old-style doctor who "knows" what he is doing.*

84.  INT. LARGE BEAUTY PARLOR, LONG SLOW PAN, showing the rear view of a long line of hair dryers;  as the CAMERA passes each dryer we will catch a snatch of conversation from the occupant, unseen, of course. The row of ladies will be designated by numbers.

### NUMBER ONE (v.o.)
...only amusing myself, naturally, haven't really played for years . But Genevieve gives me this smile. "Mother!" You know- butter wouldn't melt!  Which means watch out!  Two seconds later- the guillotine! There are two things a lady <u>can't</u> do with crossed legs, Mother, she says.  One, play the violin!...

### NUMBER TWO (v.o.)
...but you're really going to put her on the pill? Fourteen years of age?...

53

### NUMBER THREE (v.o.)
...listen, why kid ourselves? The last time Maureen
and I had one of our heart- to - hearts, she took a bottle from her
handbag. "Try my brand," she says, "they're much better."
Between the eye shadow and the lipstick!  In her handbag!...

### NUMBER FOUR (v.o.)
...the reason people are afraid to be naked, Cynthia,
is because they think they have too much or too little to show.
                      (*revelatory*)
                      (*continued*)

84. Cont.

### NUMBER FOUR (v.o.- continued)
...I tell you after we were all undressed in the pool, holding hands
like little children - I felt I knew for the first time what trust - real
trust - really and truly meant!...

### NUMBER FIVE (v.o.)
...Okay, so she had a breast removed!  Does that give her the right
to tell me how to bring up $mY$ own children? ...

### NUMBER SIX (v.o.)
...three-twenty?  Just to have some half naked slob of
a so-called actor--- allergic to soap, this I can testify to-- leap into
your lap? I mean, talk about nerve!...

### NUMBER SEVEN (v.o.)
...I decided on rust, I'm mad about rust...

### NUMBER EIGHT (v.o.)
...snored through the first half of the film, naturally. Okay. Then
objected , it was in Swedish.  Then complained he forgot his gas
pills. I'm wet all over it's so sexy, - all he can think is where are my
gas pills!...

### NUMBER NINE (v.o.)
...maybe we'll just sell the house and rent.
Now that the children are gone...

### NUMBER TEN (v.o.)
...Jung said it once and for all, Marian. "Like wine
we are bom in a given place at a given time and like wine, quite
naturally, we bear the marks of our origins."  So if you want to
argue, don't argue with me, go argue with Jung!...

*CAMERA MOVES FORWARD past the last dryer, on to the face of a dandified, mustachioed BEAUTICIAN in his 30's, broadly grinning, holding up a mirror in front of him.*

### BEAUTICIAN
**Presto! Out of the cocoon. Behold, Mrs. McAlister! How's that for a resurrection!**

DISSOLVE:

---

84.    *INT. BAR-FAIRLY STYLISH HOTEL. MEDIUM CLOSE- WOMAN- her mid-40's, well-dressed, intelligent, but drinking too much. She puts down her glass. She looks up, her face is tear stained. She is in the midst of a confessional to Helen, who's next to her, listening.*

### WOMAN
**...So then he gets this bug. Suddenly: twin beds! After twenty years! But okay! Humor the man! And guess what? In no time those twin beds became- I don't know- Berlin, east and west! I mean, if you wanted to cross you had to practically apply for a goddam visa!**
*(she gulps her drink; obviously drinking too much)*
**So then the usual. Honestly, it's so boring I'd fall asleep if I didn't feel like jumping out of the window!**
*(she sips again)*
**At the Shoreham on Somerset, Isobel saw him pawing a young thing, sandaled, twenty-one if a day! And wearing one of those, you know, venetian blind jobs , where the nipples play peek-a-boo every time you move.**
*(nervously lights a Cigarette)*
**Right away- excuse the pun -I decided: tit for tat! So two days later I met an Air Force type. He was shopping , he paid me the compliment to think I was selling .**
*(big sigh)*
**I thought, you know, what the hell, tea and sympathy , maybe I was curious, besides, believe me, I could use the money.**
*(continued)*

85.  Cont.

### WOMAN (continued)
*(dramatic revelation)*
**But nothing! Zero! The whole time I kept seeing that big slob's**

**face. God help me, I still love the man, maybe it's because I know what all his pills are for.**

(*a peroration*)

**I mean, let's face it, with you it's very different, Helen. You're a very brainy woman. You live on a different level entirely ... But with me, with an ordinary person like me...?**

<u>WAITER (v.o.)</u>
**Excuse me, ladies.**

CAMERA PULLS BACK to include BAR MAN who has a tray with two glasses of champagne, which he places on cocktail table.

<u>BAR MAN</u>
**Compliments of the two gentlemen at the end of the bar.**

*86.        On TWO NAVAL OFFICERS sitting at the bar. They raise their glasses in a toast TO CAMERA , smiling. CAMERA MOVES FORWARD between them, as bar man switches on television set, an over-large screen attached to the ceiling .*

86.        On the TV: a crowd of students, chanting, pass by on the screen, which is now at a CLOSE ANGLE.  They carry signs which are visible, each held up for a few seconds : (there is a festive OFF-STAGE SOUND, an amateur rock band, which continues through most of this scene)

**"We Know That We Shall Never See! A Smokestack Lovely As A Tree!" ... "Green Power. Hallelujah, <u>Equals Life Power!</u>" ... "The Earth Is The Lord's And The Fullness Thereof! (But The Garbage Is Strictly <u>Our</u> Own Idea!)" ... "Life Expectancy Of Words We Could Do Without- "CONFRONTATION " - Eleven Mos.-"POLARIZATION"-Ten Mos.-"ECOLOGY"-???????."**

*87.        A telephoto shot high up atop a redwood tree: RO is distinctly and shockingly visible sitting in the Lotus position, bare to the waist, tan, smiling, very calm...*

88.        Line of campus cops along the roadway, not angry, facing the good-natured heckling of the kids O.S.

89.        Inside the previous Bar scene: The  two Naval Officers, whom
90.        we've  seen previously. BUT NOT HELEN HERSELF- Her attention is now riveted to the TV screen, watching .

**STUDENT (v.o.)**
**Since the Dean refused to meet with us today , we've had to
invent a Dean of our own.  Hello there, Dean.**

91.     Television set- CLOSE UP.  On an image of a student- tall, rangy,
        bespectacled, and  wearing  a broad diagonal sash, which has
        painted on it the single word: **Dean.**

**STUDENT DEAN**
*(full of facetious ingratiation)*
**Hello there, Young Person... I just want to say I'm not one of those
who decry- in fact I applaud -the concerns of Young People. I
admire Young People. I think we have to pay serious attention to
what Young People are trying to tell us.**

**STUDENT (v.o.)**
**For instance, quit black-topping the grass?**

92.     *Construction trucks on road as several hard-hated workers
        jump off, lugging huge chain saws.*

91.  Cont.

**STUDENT (v.o.)**
**Quit cutting down trees?
Putting up power plants to foul up the area?**

92.     *On Ro, atop the tree. He doesn't budge. He looks down,
        and then up again.*

**STUDENT DEAN (v.o.)**
*(conceding the sorrowful facts of life)*
**Young  Person- you know as well as I--there's a difference between
*des*tructive and *cons*tructive criticism, - right?**

93.     *ANOTHER ANGLE . The road area.  Showing cops moving
        away, construction workers moving in toward the trees, their
        chain saws at the ready.*

**STUDENT DEAN (v.o.)**
*(pedagogic)*
**I mean, this whole project has been thoroughly studied,
researched, reviewed, etcetera!**

94.     Television screen. There is a placard held up by a student,
        CLOSE UP.  It bears the following crayoned lines:

57

**"There is an entire semantics ready to deal with this sort of thing - it involves such phrases as Those Are The Facts...We are under repeated pressure to accept things presented to us as *already settled ...*" - George Wald.**

## STUDENT DEAN (v.o.)
**After all, facts are facts ...**

95.      Portion of the bar, looking, Helen excluded, of course.

## STUDENT CHANT (v.o.)
**"Nous sommes tous- des juifs allemands!"**
**(*We're all German Jews!*)**

*At this point there is, O.S., the terrible , brutal- and, alas, common as dirt- SOUND of the chain saws, beginning to bite into living wood. This rasp, this brutal whine, will continue to the very end of this scene, in crescendo, together with the continual periodic chant of the students.*

96.      Television set. Another placard held up before the CAMERA. On it is written, also in crayoned free-hand printing:

**"Nous sommes tous des juifs allemands!**
**(We are all German Jews!")**

French Students Chant , Paris. May 1968.

97.      *RO, atop his tree, looking down.*

98.      Hard-hatted workman wrestling his chain saw at the foot of Ro's tree, as it bites into the wood .

99.      *On Helen's friend, looking up ,startled: there is the SOUND of another person, O.S., jumping up, a DOOR SLAMMING. A woman's high heeled shoes running.*

100.    *EXT. CITY STREET. A bus-load of soldiers passing. They slowly wheel before our gaze and out. (NOTE : it is very important that during the buildup of sequence of images now, we have the sound straight there is the student chant which we heard before- Nous sommes tous des ju ifs allemands- combined with the growing crescendo of the chain saws , by now malevolent choir. And at the same time there is the helter*

*skelter rat-a-tat-tat of a woman's shoes, fleeing on city pavements- Helen's, of course- plus her O.S., audible, strangulated breathing. )*

101. *EXT. DEPARTMENT STORE WINDOW. We SEE escalator within, people being carried both up and down, standing, conveyed like objects on a belt.*

102. *EXT. STREET CROSSING as the light changes and a crowd of people begin rushing pell mell across, to make the light, before the carnivorous traffic mows them down.*

103. *SIGHTSEEING BUS. The passengers sit inside, glazed- we can SEE a guide with mike in hand, pointing out the sights- the passengers stare dully, they don't seem to be rejuvenated.*

104. *EXT. GATES OF CITY SWEATER FACTORY. As bunch of employees come rushing out, punching their time cards flinging themselves onto the sidewalk.*

105. *INT. RENTAL CAR SHACK. A salesman is there, feet up on*
the *little desk, cigar in mouth, glowering at his television set, which is O.S. He suddenly gets up, noticing something, and strolls to the door.*

106. *RENTAL CAR LOT. Black-topped. Cars. SOUND of Helen's*
feet *running, SOUND of her breath, anguished: SOUND of the students' chant, and that terrible inexorable burr of the chain saws. IN CAMERA, growing larger, is the sudden shocking image of the GREEN MUSTANG of the opening prologue. It grows larger and larger in view.*

As we watch the car, there is a stunning, stupefying, O.S. CRASH- inimitable sound of a tall tree toppling. This crash immediately melds into another kind of crash -the terrible and unmistakable clang of metal against metal, sound of the car accident which we first heard at the end of the prologue. The green mustang in view seems visibly to shake under the impact. Suddenly superimposed upon it, larger than life- size now- is the image of the shattered dashboard clock at the end of the prologue sequence, glass broken, hands arrested at five minutes to twelve. All sounds instantly die away- shocking interval of silence.

# CANCER

"CONJUNCTIONS FAVORABLE FOR NEW CONTACT
— LEAVE WORDLY AFFAIRS ALONE. NOW IS THE
TIME TO PLAY CLOSE ATTENTION TO
*INTIMATE* MATTERS."

107.   A BATHROOM SINK MIRROR.  On Nicholas McAllister:
       dressed in pajamas, a book propped up in front of him, at the
       moment gargling vigorously.

108.   BEDROOM: showing Helen McAllister at her dressing table. In
       B.G. a television set is going, a droning weather report. Helen is
       using a skin vibrator on her face, a practiced and expert
       maneuver.

### NICHOLAS (v.o.)
**Where shall the word be found, where will the word resound?**
**Not here-**

109.   On Nicholas entering bathroom. He is begins using a water
       pick, spraying the inside of his mouth.

### NICHOLAS (v.o.)
**"...there is not enough silence, the right time an**
**the right place are not here..."**

Nicholas finishes with the water pick, starts to go O.S.

110.   INT. BEDROOM, as Nicholas comes out of the bathroom, going
about his nightly chores : we are in, of course, the nightly ballet of the
middle-aged going-to-bed routine. In B.G. now is another SOUND, a
foot vibrator. Nicholas turns down thermostat, raises the blinds, goes
o.s. to shut off TV. Lose Nicholas, CAMERA STAYS on bureau,
SLOWLY PANNING a series of framed photographs: Nicholas as a
young Divinity School graduate; Nicholas and Helen newly married;
young couple, with one small daughter, standing in front of modest
church; Nicholas dedicating stone of a new building; Nicholas and Helen
as they are now, dressed in conventional finery, standing in front of
magnificent new church.

As this PAN of photographs slowly scans the images, we continue to
hear Nicholas' VOICE.

111.  Cont.

### NICHOLAS (v.o.)
*(eloquent, vaguely echoing)*
**"Oh, perpetual recurrence of predetermined seasons ...world**
**of spring and autumn, birth and dying..."**

112.     On large double bed. Helen is already in it, not asleep, waiting.
CAMERA CLOSES IN on her a little: her face pensive, not too
expectant.

**NICHOLAS (v.o.)**
**"Where is the life...lost in living?"**

*Nicholas comes INTO SHOT and gets into bed with a book; kisses his
wife in a comradely manner and takes up a study of the pages,
absorbed.*

**NICHOLAS (v.o.)**
**"Where is the wisdom... lost in knowledge?"**

*Helen sighs, turns off her night light, turns on her side and tries to go to
sleep. Nicholas continues to read, his night light still on.*

**NICHOLAS (v.o.)**
**"The cycles of heaven in twenty centuries, bring us farther from
God and neared to the dust..."**

DISSOLVE:

---

113.     EXT. MAGNIFICENT NEW EPISCOPAL CHURCH, in a
suburban neighborhood . As Nicholas comes out of the front alone,
CAMERA PANNING him over to the permanent announcement placard
in front of the church. CLOSE SHOT announcement placard. It reads:
**"SUNDAY WORSHIP, 10 A.M. N.D. McALLISTER.  TEXT : WISDOM
OF T.S. ELLIOT ."**

114.     INT. WAITING CAR, its motor running.  Helen is seated there,
dressed stylishly, waiting.  As Nicholas slips under the wheel,
smiles at her, and starts to drive away.

**NICHOLAS (v.o.)**
**"I journeyed  to London, the time kept city..."**

115.     LARGE URBAN BOULEVARD -like La Cienega in LA. Bordered
by lots of restaurants. A ROAR of traffic.

**NICHOLAS (v.o.)**
**"Where the river flows..."**

116.    SLOW PAN.  A cluster, a veritable cabal- of architecturally over-dressed restaurants facades, also ala La Cienega.

NICHOLAS (v.o.)
**"There I was told, we have too many churches, and too few chop houses."**

117.    **INT. CAR**.  On Nicholas and Helen. Nicholas is shaving with a plug-in electric razor, temporarily halted in traffic : Helen is assiduously making up her face.

HELEN (v.o.)
**How about roast veal?  Braised kidneys?
Stewed iguana?**

NICHOLAS (v.o.)
**Fine, my dear.**

HELEN (v.o.)
**Nicholas!  Please! The menu! The goddam day-after-day rain-or-shine til death-us-do-part menu!**

NICHOLAS (v.o.)
**Whatever appeals to you...**

HELEN (v.o.)
(*a sudden slash*)
**If it appeals to you, it'll appeal to me! Deuce, thirty all, your serve!  Okay?**

*At this point, Nicholas puts away his razor, Helen snaps her pocketbook shut, the car shoots ahead; they are not looking at one another, staring at the roadway.*

DISSOLVE:

---

*118.    INT. BANQUET HALL- WALL. There is a large blown-up and quite horrible photograph of Hiroshima being pulverized by the bomb. On either side are two flags, United States and Japanese. Beneath the photograph is printed placard, stark ,in dripping letters, that is, in letters dripping as if they were seeping blood. The placard reads:*

**"8:15AM- AUGUST 6, 1945."** Underneath this placard one other, reading: **"IN MEMORIAM."**

118. Cont.
*CAMERA MOVES from wall, slowly down head table: we are at a Hiroshima memorial meeting. A small JAPANESE is on his feet, talking; he is very scarred, bent, gnarled- a terrifying visual apostrophe to the brutality of the bomb. During the subsequent V.O. dialogue, CAMERA WILL PAN slowly down table, showing seated guests listening, on each plate crossed Japanese and American flags; at the very end we will reach Nicholas and Helen, HOLD for a second, then SLOWLY PAN BACK til we end up on the terrible picture of the bomb burst; all this, of course, will have to be sensitively timed. Meanwhile we HEAR the following voices.*

**HELEN (v.o.)**
Please Nicko. Just once?

**NICHOLAS (v.o.)**
No.

**HELEN (v.o.)**
If I smile wickedly?

**NICHOLAS (v.o.)**
Look, I'm a pajama reactionary.  If you want to sleep
nude- by all means, sleep nude.

**HELEN (v.o.)**
It'll be good for you.

**NICHOLAS (v.o.)**
I'm sure. But not for my - excuse the term - post nasal drip.

**HELEN (v.o.)**
Ah, you're turning into a party pooper, Nicholas! A post nasal S.D.-
for Sex Dropout - party pooper drip!

**NICHOLAS (v.o.)**
What's this bill from Wallington's?  Hundred and twelve dollars,
- pane of glass?

**HELEN (v.o.)**
Mirror. I'd like a mirror on the ceiling.

NICHOLAS (v.o.)
Why?

HELEN (v.o.)
Come here. I can't say why out loud. It's just a nasty little trick
out of the women's mags.

NICHOLAS (v.o.)
Here's that quote from Kiergegaard I was looking for. *"We're
all in the wrong where God's concerned* ." Remember?

HELEN (v.o.)
Dear, counselor, who can I sue? Kiergegaard? The apostles?
St. John of the Cross? My husband's lousy imitation of Miss
Lonelyhearts?

119.    CLOSE SHOT- TV SCREEN: Nicholas is disclosed, sitting
before a table in front of three telephones. A blackboard behind him.
Very harassed. He is speaking, passionately, on the phone.

NICHOLAS
...obviously you wanted help, Gerald, or you wouldn't have
called - right? I mean, don't cop out now! Besides, there are plenty
of people waiting to get through, just as up tight are you
are! Now I want to know what was in those pills and how long
before- hello?
(he hangs up, disgusted to audience)
We'll have to try to trace the number.  Get on it, Majorie!
(he picks up another phone)
Father Nicholas...Wait, I can't understand a word unless you
stop crying...

120.    *INT. HOSPITAL WARD. On Helen, dressed as a grey lady. She
is standing, hand on hip, bemusedly watching the television set O.S. A
quizzical expression on her face.*

120.  Cont.
NICHOLAS (v.o.- on TV)
Nobody's going to judge you, nobody cares. You can believe in the
devil, the Lochness monster, or even Brier Rabbit...okay, I'll take
my collar off. Better?

121.    TELEVISION SCREEN. On Nicholas, as he suddenly tears his
        clerical collar off and hurls it on the table, peering out at the
        audience, the phone in his hand.

122.    INT. ART GALLERY. TWO SHOT: Helen and Nicholas, dressed
        in their ceremonial finery. They are looking O.S., waiting for a
        speech to end; ready to unveil a prize painting . Nicholas' right
        arm, upraised, holds a sash.

**HELEN (v.o.)**
**My God, when you threw your collar;**
**my old ladies nearly had a heart attack!**

**NICHOLAS (v.o.)**
**I had to.  She sounded like she was going over the hill...**

**HELEN (v.o.)**
*(with good natured maliciousness)*
**If you'd only taken off your halo at the same time! ...**

Nicholas, responding to an O.S. signal, pulls the sash. There is a burst
of applause O.S. CAMERA MOVES UP, losing Helen and Nicholas.
centering now on a statue decorated with a prize ribbon. It is the Christ,
very modish, a black flower child, bent on the rack, flower in hand, long
curly hair, blue jeans, bare feet, tears are visible on his cheek, frozen of
course. He wears an old World War I jacket, blood encrusted. A vaguely
campy air.

DISSOLVE:

---

123.    EXT.CHURCH PLACARD. It reads: **GUEST SPEAKER: PRIZE**
        **WINNI NG ARTIST - MOHAMMED AHMAN . TOPIC- THE**
        **FIRST BLACK MILITANT - BIRTHPLACE : GALILEE!**

123. Cont.

**NICHOLAS (v.o.)**
**"The desert is not remote in the southern tropics ..."**

124.    INT. CHURCH PULPIT. A BLACK MAN talking - in fact,
        enraged. He is shaking his finger at the congregation. He
        wears, of course, long robes, a Moslem fez; he is giving the
        congregation hell, as might be expected.

#### NICHOLAS (v.o.)
**"The desert is not only around the corner..."**

SLOW PAN, left of pulpit: the prize winning statue draped, placed on a pedestal, is now centered in CAMERA .

#### NICHOLAS (v.o.)
**"The desert is squeezed in the tube train next to you..."**

PAN on Helen and Nicholas, seated, listening. They pretend to be absorbed; a certain distraction, however, disfigures their faces.

#### NICHOLAS (v.o .)
**"The desert is in the heart of your brother..."**

ZOOM IN for MEDIUM CLOSE on Helen and Nicholas.

#### HELEN (v .o.)
**If we lose Louise, it will be your fault,...**

#### NICHOLAS (v.o.)
**Why should we lose Louise?**

125.      EXT. CHURCH- DAY. On Nicholas and Helen. They are shaking hands, with departing parishioners. Their faces are set with smiles. The organ is BOOMING somewhere inside. We don't see the parishioners, of course, only a succession of hands being clasped .

#### HELEN (v.o.)
**One more of those death row smiles when she brings in dinner ...**

125.  Cont.

#### NICHOLAS (v.o.)
**It's a defect, agreed . But I wilt at the  sight of fried brains ...**

DISSOLVE

126.     *INT. PULPIT. On Nicholas, CLOSE ANGLE . He is dressed in clerical robes, gravely sprinkling holy water on something O.S. SOUND of a baby squalling somewhere nearby. Nicholas gravely makes the sign of the cross - obviously he is presiding at a baptismal.*

#### HELEN (v.o.)
...for which she happens to be famous throughout
the solar system...

#### NICHOLAS (v.o.)
And which you didn't so much as hint at...

#### HELEN (v.o.)
Correction - which I did! Only you didn't pay attention! As usual!

127.    INT. PULPIT. MEDIUM CLOSE on Nicholas. He is dressed in
        black robes. He comes up to the empty altar. Organ in
        background SOFTLY PLAYING.

#### NICHOLAS
Let us pray...

128.    EXT. CHURCH ANNOUNCEMENT PLACARD. It reads:
"FUNERAL SERVICES, J.L. BERNARD. TEXT:
WISDOM OF B. FULLER, MODERN PROPHET."

#### NICHOLAS (v.o.)
God, it seems to me
Is a verb...
Not a noun, proper or improper...

129.    EXT. CEMETARY PATH- MOVING. On Nicholas and Helen,
somberly dressed, trotting the graveled path, behind a line of mourners
who themselves are O.S.

#### NICHOLAS (v.o.)
"Is loving, Not the abstraction "love"
Commanded or entreated..."

130.    GRAVE SITE. It is a butte, overlooking the ocean below. As
Nicholas and Helen gravely walk INTO SCENE and stop, heads slightly
bowed. SOUND O.S. of funeral cortege, etc.

#### NICHOLAS (v.o.)
"Not legislative code, Not proclamation law, Not academic dogma,
Not ecclesiastic canon..."

*Here CHOIR begins to SING, O.S., any one of the proper Episcopal hymns- "Nearer My God To Thee" perhaps. Nicholas' and Helen's faces have expressions of intent abstraction ; after all, they have gone through this rite many times before. ZOOM IN to CLOSE on their faces.*

131.    REVERSE LONG ANGLE from their POV-
        the ocean down below.

<u>NICHOLAS (v.o.)</u>
**Hey, I just got a food flash: fish!**

<u>HELEN (v.o.)</u>
*(equally conspiratorial, whispering)*
**What?**

<u>NICHOLAS (v.o.)</u>
**I said fish!**

<u>HELEN (v.o.)</u>
**Fish?**

<u>NICHOLAS (v.o.)</u>
**F-i-s-h.  Fish.  What's wrong with fish?**

<u>DISSOLVE:</u>

---

132.    INT. HELEN AND NICHOLAS' CAR- MOVING.  Both dressed
as      before.  Nicholas driving .

<u>HELEN</u>
**Nicholas?**

132.  Cont.

<u>NICHOLAS</u>
**Hmmm?**

<u>HELEN</u>
**What kind of fish?**

### NICHOLAS
**Any kind!  What's the difference?  I just feel like fish, that's all!**

### DISSOLVE:

---

133.    INT. NICHOLAS' AND HELEN'S BEDROOM.  On Helen, seated on the bed, a drink in her hand, dressed in a slip. Obviously she has had several drinks already. In B.G. Nicholas is taking off his clerical habit.

### HELEN
(*a little tipsy*)
**Now then!  Let's see what the letter "S" has to offer...**
(*she thinks, concentrating*)
**Squid?  You throw up! Sea bass?  Cholesterol!  Shrimp?
Uh uh!
Too chummy with plankton.
Which is too chummy with OTT.  Salmon?...**

### NICHOLAS
(*as he comes forward, Exasperated, dressed in a robe*)
**Forget it! Obviously you don't want fish-**

### HELEN
(*sweetly*)
**I want what you want, dear.**

### NICHOLAS
(*acid*)
**You want to pick a fight - that's what you want!**

He exits into bathroom. She sits there. She is silent. She looks at her image in a bureau mirror against the near wall.

133.  Cont.

### HELEN
(*rollicking*)
**"Mirror, mirror on the wall, Do I really reek of gall?"**
(*calling towards the bathroom*)
**You're right!  I'm a bitch, Nicholas!**
(*beginning to dial the phone, somewhat confusedly,
on the bedside table*)

71

**A rum dum querulous dehydrated -**
*(she stops, confused, can't remember) ...*

Nicholas comes back to the room, towel over his arm,
to get some toilet articles .

### HELEN
*(continuing)*
**I forget Carol's area code?**

### NICHOLAS
*(very brisk, and sardonic)*
**At half past four A.M. Tokyo time?**

He exits again to bathroom.

### HELEN
*(as she dials another number, slowly yet not too precisely)*
**You are mean, Father Nicholas, his bitchy wife said...
if only you'd visit, *my* side of the bed!**
*(she puts the phone on the amplifier)*

### PHONE
**The temperature outside is 67 degrees-**

*She suddenly hangs up the phone with a BANG. She drains the rest of
her drink. She contemplates herself a little unsteadily in the mirror.*

134.     MIRROR, as Helen talks to her own image, gravely, yet tipsily,
         philosophic.

### HELEN
**God bless Helen. And God bless her impacted wisdom tooth. And
God bless Nicholas . And God bless his post nasal drip. And God
bless the Church of our Lady. And God bless her post nasal-**

134.     INT. BATHROOM.  On Nicholas, as he starts in with the water
         pick routine.

### HELEN (v.o.)
**Help! Nickol Fire!**

*At that he turns, bolts for the bedroom.*

135.     *INT. BEDROOM as Nicholas comes rushing in, to find Helen*

*standing there, posing; she has on a little black lacy negligee .
She pirouettes, turns, smiles.*

### HELEN
**Well, what else could I yell? With this on?**

*Nicholas turns, proceeds back to bathroom.  Helen following.*

### HELEN
*(a note of entreaty)*
**Nicko...**

136.    *INT. BATHROOM.  On Nicholas, as he comes to the mirror,
poking at one eye with a finger.*

### NICHOLAS
*(turning to Helen, Kleenex in his hand)*
**Here. Something in my eye.  It's all blurred.**

*She comes to him, sits him gravely down on the bathtub edge, seats
herself deliberately on his lap, begins gently to dab at his eye.*

### HELEN
*(gentle mimicry)*
**"It's all blurred..."  Now that's what the
kids call "relevant philosophy!"**

137. *Cont. (another tone, bending closer)*
**Did you know, Father, that after 40 the sexual relationship
can achieve Even Greater Richness than Ever Before?  Also,
it's very helpful for the wife to Take The Initiative?  Also, a
change of locale is Sometimes Conducive?**

*She throws the Kleenex away. She deliberately bends over him,
pressing herself against him, her mouth to his. After a second,*
*he* *responds ...embraced, they slowly tumble back into the empty
bathtub.*

DISSOLVE:

---

137.   INT. BATHROOM, on Helen, alone in bathtub, disconsolately staring out, elbows propped up on the side. She sighs. Blows her hair a little. Nicholas is nowhere to be seen.

### HELEN
**All right!  At least we know- bathtubs are *not* conducive ...!**

She climbs out of bathtub, begins to wash up in front of the mirror: during subsequent dialogue she will wash and dry her face, use the water pick - usual nightly ablutions.

### HELEN
*(loud voice, calling to other room)*
**I  read about this clinic in Romania, Nicko. They do fantastic things. 80 year olds chasing teenage nurses through the corridors, etcetera. Two injections a week , - eleven different flavors of Yogurt!**
*(arch)*
**You <u>are</u> crazy about Yogurt - right?**
*(she stares at herself in bathroom mirror)*

**Babies!  Face it, we should have had seven!
Adopted or not; I don't care!**

138.   Cont.
*(she begins to hum a little to herself)*
**"Black, black, black, is the color- "**
*(addressing herself sternly)*
**Why not Africa? I mean, so many babies in...**
*(now she is toweling herself, turning back
toward the bedroom;  calling to her husband)*
**Remember Bergman's Magician," Nicko?  The old man dying because his prayers weren't answered? "Use me,- dear God - use me!"**
*(another tone)*
*(continued)*

### HELEN
*(continued)*
**I pray all the time, and what do I get?  Agenda of Good Deeds? Difficulty in telling what day it is?**
*(she starts out toward the bedroom)*
**"Use me!...**

139.   BEDROOM, as Helen enters, Nicholas nowhere to be seen.

## HELEN
*(continuing)*
**At my age, it's a crime- right? I mean, simply to drift without-**
*She sees something on her pillow, goes over to it, picks up a book - obviously left there for her. She looks at it.*

140.    CLOSE SHOT- book title: "Schedule of Courses . Fall Term. Graduate Division. Requirements for Advanced Degrees- Academy of Arts and Letters."

141.    MEDIUM CLOSE on Helen: bemused, looking O.S.; taking this suggestion thoughtfully in.

### DISSOLVE:

---

142.    EXT.CHURCH PLACARD. It reads: **"SUNDAY WORSHIP. 10 AM. N.D. McALLISTER. TEXT: WISDOM OF C. LEVY-STRAUSS , FRENCH ANTHROPOLGIST ."**

143.    *INT. NICHOLAS' STUDY.  On Nicholas, pacing back and forth, pipe in his mouth;  he settles down to a desk piled with books and papers, begins to copy with a pen from one of the books open before him.*

## NICHOLAS (v.o.)
**"The camp fires shine out..."**

(NOTE: the following sequence of shots will be taken from STOCK FOOTAGE. In black and white. Very grainy, and perhaps with an amateur, awkward rhythm to it-the kind of amateur film frequently brought back by anthropologists from their primitive safaris. We will also hear the SOUND of a 16mm projector running O.S.)

144.    A TRACT OF LOOK-ALIKE SUBURBAN HOUSING- NIGHT. Lights on in many of the windows.

144.    Cont.

## NICHOLAS (v.o.)
**"...in the darkened savannah ..."**

145.    INT. BAR- Circular- the usual resort flotsam, seated, drinking .

75

> **NICHOLAS (v.o.)**
> "...around the heath which is their."

146.     ANOTHER BAR- more of the same.

> **NICHOLAS (v.o.)**
> "...only protection from the cold..."

147.     INT. HOTEL LOBBY showing a row of tropical plants, infant palms in buckets, backed by plastic flowers.

> **NICHOLAS (v.o.)**
> "...behind the flimsy screen of foliage and palm leaves..."

CAMERA MOVES UP to show plants and trees stuffed in buckets on a polished cement floor.

> **NICHOLAS (v.o.)**
> "...stuck into the ground..."

148.     SUPERMARKET CHECK OUT COUNTER. Showing the usual incredible pile of groceries stuffed into the wire baskets.

> **NICHOLAS (v.o.)**
> "...besides the baskets ..."

149.     BEACH SCENE- NOON. Crowded with families, loaded down with all the paraphernalia we bring to the beach: snorkels, magazines, surf riders, swim fins, transistor radios, etc.

> **NICHOLAS (v.o.)**
> "...filled with the pitiable objects..."

150.     TRAILER CAMP. Big mobile homes, parked like elephants, surrounded by their umbilical cords, pumps, air compressors, gas tanks, cables to water, etc.

150.  Cont.

> **NICHOLAS (v.o.)**
> "...which comprise all their earthly belongings ..."

151.     FAMILY GROUPS ON BEACH- a LONGER ANGLE, showing more of the crowd.

**NICHOLAS (v.o.)**
**"...the Nambikwara lie on the bare earth..."**

152.     GROUP OF POLICEMEN outside a Chicago courthouse,
         riot clothes on, helmeted, booted, braced.

**NICHOLAS (v.o.)**
**"...always, of course, haunted by the thought of other groups..."**

153.     ON TV SCREEN, VICE PRESIDENT AGNEW, orating,
         gesticulating vigorously .

154.     GROUP OF BLACK PANTHERS, in their arrogant public strut.
         Bereted, armed, grim-faced- guarding an old store front which is
         their headquarters .

**NICHOLAS (v.o.)**
**"...as fearful ..."**

155.     WOMEN'S LIBERATION GROUP, with pickets and signs;
parading up and down at a burlesque house. Ranting to passers-by.

**NICHOLAS (v.o.)**
**"...and as hostile..."**

156.     *GRIM GROUP OF ARAB DELEGATES TO U.N., distinctly*
*recognizable ,with kafir and cape, striding through a belligerent crowd,*
*howling abuse- shock troops from a New York ghetto .*

**NICHOLAS (v.o.)**
**"...as themselves ..."**

157.     A QUEUE OF COUPLES lined up for their turn at rollercoaster
         in amusement park.

**NICHOLAS (v.o.)**
**"...but when they lined up, entwined together,**
**couple by couple..."**

158.     ELDERLY COUPLE, shrieking with fear and joy in a
         rollercoaster gondola, clutching hold of one another.

**NICHOLAS (v.o.)**
**"...each looking to his mate for support and comfort..."**

159.    *ANOTHER COUPLE, perhaps younger, in amusement park dodgem cars, squealing, banging against another car with another couple.*

### NICHOLAS (v.o.)
**"...and finds in the other a bulwark - perhaps the only one known..."**

160.    A GREAT FREEWAY AT NIGHT, absolutely jammed, hardly moving, acres of cars.

**161.**   TWO GREAT BULLDOZERS, gauging out earth from a suburban countryside. Nearby a sign:
**NEW HOME OF YOUR FRIENDLY NEIGHBORHOOD SAFEWAY.**

### NICHOLAS (v.o.)
**"...against the problems..."**

162.    ON HIGHWAY SOMEWHERE , group of vagabond hippies, they stand grinning; they hold up a sign- behind them their VW busses parked. The sign reads: **ANY DOPE TO SELL?**

163.    NEWSPAPER PHOTOGRAPH OF A GENERAL, generously bedecked with medals. Caption reads:
**WAR ULTIMATE TEST OF NATION'S MORAL FIBER, GENERAL DECLARES .**

### NICHOLAS (v.o.)
**"...and difficulties of every day..."**

164.    PAN: SERIES OF GROUP SHOTS- couples, family groups, children- collected in various rooms, seated, dulled after hours of TV watching, staring at their carnivorous screen.

### NICHOLAS(v .o.)
**"...plus the meditative melancholia which from time to time overwhelms the Nambikwara ..."**

165.    *TV SCREEN- On Nicholas CLOSE UP. He is pleading. We don't HEAR any sound. He seems exhausted. He throws off his collar, then his coat, phones are ringing- though, of course, still no sound. He is speaking on two at once, then picks up another receiver, a hand hands him another...*

HELEN (v.o.)
**Nicko!...Nicko! ...**

166.   *INT. NICHOLAS' STUDY - EARLY EVENING. TWO SHOT on Nicholas and Helen. He is seated at his desk, books all around, very disheveled, obviously just woken up. Helen stands in front, dressed in street clothes, school books under her arm. She has, obviously, just shaken him into wakefulness.*

HELEN
**The time is twenty-two and a half past seven!
PM! "Courtesy of Zion Bible Institute!"**

NICHOLAS
*(sleepily)*
**Why so late?**

HELEN
*(seating herself on his lap)*
**Oh, you'll admire me, I'm very brilliant, I got stuck in a ditch, the Auto Club had to bail me out ...**
*(she produces a photograph from within one of her books)*
**But look - consolation prize!**

167.   CLOSE - on the original Polaroid print of the spider web, which we, of course, have already seen.

HELEN (v.o.)
**I met a student. I mean, a *student* student!
Yoga, yin, yang, Zodiac is Destiny -the works!**

168.   NICHOLAS AND HELEN, studying the photograph.

HELEN
*(indicating the picture)*
**This - believe it or not- was his sole project for the afternoon.**

NICHOLAS
**Even <u>after</u> you came along?**

168.  Cont.

HELEN
**Come on! I couldn't compete with anything like that!**

79

NICHOLAS
(*yawning, stretching his arms*)
**I'm hungry, let's go out.**

HELEN
(*saucily*)
**How about ... Fish?**

*They look at each other; they burst out laughing.*

DISSOLVE:

--------------------------------------------------

169.    INT. INTIMATE RESTAURANT. Showing Helen and Nicholas at
        table. She is very animated, gesticulating a mile a minute.
        Obviously telling everything that has happened to her- that is,
        not quite everything, of course.

NICHOLAS (v.o.)
**Why spoil it for you, my dear?**

DISSOLVE

170.    *EXT. BOULEVARD- MOVING. The two of them strolling along.
        She is still enthusiastically talking, he gravely listening, smoking his
        pipe.*

NICHOLAS (v.o.)
**After all, you seemed so rejuvenated...**

DISSOLVE:

--------------------------------------------------

171.    *INT. THEIR BEDROOM.  He is watching, amused. She is
        showing him, as a joke, a certain clumsy Yoga position...*

NICHOLAS (v.o.)
**So beloved among the sons and daughters, as it were of our
privileged congregation...**

172.  *INT. BREAKFAST TABLE. Both finishing breakfast. She looks at her watch, grabs her books, kisses Nicholas, and runs out. He smiles after her.*

**NICHOLAS (v.o.)**
**... who had just that afternoon ...**

173.  *INT. NICHOLAS' STUDY. He sits there. THE BISHOP, an august, elderly personage, is walking up and down, tea cup in hand, shaking his head, gesticulating.*

**NICHOLAS (v.o.)**
**...through our apologetic Bishop, of course, ---handed me another five point indictment. ..**

*The Bishop shakes hands, takes his leave. Nicholas turns back, alone at his desk, pipe in his mouth, studying books and papers.*

**NICHOLAS (v.o.)**
**One: I was too aloof...**

174.  NEGRO PRIZE WINNING PAINTER, dressed in Moslem robes.

**NICHOLAS (v.o.)**
**Two: I was too "ecumenical" ...**

175.  EXT. CHURCH PLACARD- same sign we saw earlier, which read: **SUNDAY WORSHIP, 10 AM. N.D. McALLISTER. TEXT : WISDOM OF T.S. ELLIOT.**

**NICHOLAS (v.o.)**
**Three: I was too "literary"...**

176.  *NICHOLAS ON TV- also as we saw him earlier, phone in hand, perhaps throwing off his clerical collar.*

**NICHOLAS (v.o.)**
**Four: I was too "therapeutic" ...**

177.  *INT. NICHOLAS' STUDY. As he gets up from his chair and paces up and down, very intent.*

177. Cont.
## NICHOLAS (v.o.)
**Five: I was too presumptuous. A sort of self- appointed ersatz Issiah. Inventing a wilderness to preach in that wasn't really there!**

178.   INT. CHURCH PULPIT. Nicholas, standing behind altar. A small screen is set up next to him- appropriate for showing slides. He looks at the congregation for a second, which is, of course, O.S.

## NICHOLAS
**Responsive reading, New Gospel, according to William Blake, Born 1757, died 1827.**
*(a pause, he clears his throat)*
**"The vision of Christ.  ..."**

179.   ON THE SMALL SCREEN. A projected billboard. Christ is being painted by several sign painters. A huge placard, announcing the coming of the great crusade. (NOTE: At each slide change, there will be a definite CLICK, the kind that travelogue lecturers use to indicate change of scene.)

180.   ON SMALL SCREEN.  Mobile TV truck.  Man monitoring ...

## NICHOLAS (v.o.)
**"..that Thou dost see."**

181.   INT. MOVIE THEATRE- HUGE SCREEN.  Billy Graham's face. Monstrously blown up.  In the grip of one of his perorations.

## CONGREGATION (v.o.)
**"...is my vision's..."**

182.   *SMALL SCREEN- showing a man in an audience with a walkie-talkie. Kneeling with a suppliant who has just made a "decision for Christ."*

## CONGREGATION (v.o.)
**"...greatest en-e-my ..."**

183.   ON NICHOLAS- MEDIUM ANGLE- behind alter.

### NICHOLAS
**"Thine is the..."**

184.  *SMALL SCREEN. Showing Billy Graham, shaking hands with the President, at a prayer breakfast.*

### NICHOLAS (v.o.)
**"...friend..."**

185.  SMALL SCREEN. Billy Graham on the golf course, surrounded by a crowd of psychophants.

### NICHOLAS (v.o.)
**"...of all..."**

186.  SMALL SCREEN, at launching of a new Polaris submarine, head bowed, surrounded by dozens of Navy Brass.

### NICHOLAS (v.o.)
**"...mankind..."**

### CONGREGATION (v.o.)
**"Mine speaks in..."**

187.  SMALL SCREEN; an automobile graveyard, a huge dump, the innards of wrecked cars sticking every which way.

### CONGREGATION  (v.o.)
**"...parables ..."**

188.  STORE FRONT. Showing rifles, pistols, all kinds of ammunition in the window.

### CONGREGATION (v.o.)
**"...to the..."**

189.  STORE FRONT. A huge collection of blank TV screens, facing us, piled every which way, reflecting perhaps the people passing by.

## CONGREGATION (v.o.)
### "...blind!"

190.    INT. CHURCH.  Showing a line of pew benches, their back
        rests in F.G.  Upon each number of the pew, a small white pill
        has been placed- CAMERA PANS along this row of pills and
        comes to rest on the figure of the YOUNG MAN, about 22 years
        old, wearing a scarf wound around and hanging loose over his
        shoulder, sunglasses, second-hand trench coat.  Under one
        arm he has a folded clipboard, and from the other he is
        distributing these pills.  As CAMERA comes to him he finishes
        putting the last pill in place -there are about twenty in all- and
        steps back, satisfied, smiling.

191.    INT. NICHOLAS' STUDY. Nicholas in the middle of
        a phone conversation .

### NICHOLAS
**Look, I've got somebody waiting for me... No, course not...if you
have to stay over- stay over... But please, drive strategically. That
highway is like a commuters' bowling alley in the mornings...**

192.    INT. CHURCH. On young man, now checking items on his
        clipboard, very businesslike. He looks up as Nicholas enters.

### YOUNG MAN
**Okay, Father, everything's set.  As I said, we won't require blankets
or anything like that, I mean, we won't be here that long.**
*(he starts to move off)*
**So...**

### NICHOLAS
**Hold on. Wait a minute.**
*(sympathetically)*
**In the first place, I can't offer you sanctuary myself, unilaterally.
I mean, the building doesn't belong to me, it belongs to the
congregation...**

### YOUNG MAN
**Like evil belongs to the anti-Christ, right?**
*(more seriously, earnestly)*
**Look, Father, granted: you really come across on the tube-
charisma - resonances - everything's going for you.**

*(continued)*

84

### YOUNG MAN
(*continued*)
But squandered!  Tossed away! I mean, why bother with private hang-ups?  Anybody can get freaked out by the war, the bad vibes, the draft. Right?

(*passionately*)
What I'm offering is a whole group- twenty-one souls- willing to put their bodies on the line for what we might call biblical reasons!  Face it, what's one sacrifice worth nowadays? Nada, right?  We need Christ's by the dozens,- hundreds, maybe, - to make people recognize the predicament we're in...

(*in sober explanation*)
Think of this  great  big  lifeboat, okay? And everybody - I mean, like, everybody -is inside! And there are all these goddamn leaks - the **Birth Rate Leak**, the **Arms Race Leak**, the **Pollution Leak**. The climate Leak etcetera! And meanwhile the boat's sinking and people are, like, sitting there soaking wet! And don't even realize how high the water level is

(*another tone*)
We've put up signs all over downtown announcing our little Event. But what we want from you - because you've got the Following, right?- we want you to try to talk us out of it, like on the air. As a concept, how can it fail? I mean, people won't be able to ignore it, they'll have to pay attention! **Twenty**-one souls willing to walk to Calvary for their sakes? I don't Salvation, but at least, as a gesture, it's a beginning, right?

*He moves off towards the door, CAMERA moving with him, losing Nicholas. He throws open the door of the church. He takes out his clipboard, "checking in" a waiting line of people.*

*But these people are all imaginary;  they don't exist!*


192.  Cont.

### YOUNG MAN
Okay, everybody, watch your step,
there's a slight dip in the floor...

193.      Nicholas. He stands frozen, speechless, staring.

#### YOUNG MAN (v.o.)
**And remember, keep it clean! Sanctuary means
refuge, not refuse, right?**

*Young man now returns to make a TWO SHOT with Nicholas; he is still
engaged with his clipboard, very "businesslike". He looks up.*

#### YOUNG MAN
**In case you're worrying about, you know, fire or like that, forget it!
We took a vote, came up with these ...**
(*he shows Nicholas, in the palm of one hand, a single stark pill*)
**...clean, quick, economical.
And- if we have to use them- one to a customer.**
(*shouting directions to "group"*)
**Cool it everybody, settle down, Let's concentrate
...Rufus!...**

194.　　A portion of the empty pews, their excruciating pills in F.G.

#### YOUNG MAN (v.o.)
**...put down that joint , where in hell do you think you are!**

195.　　MEDIUM on Nicholas, speechless, still unable to move.


196.　　ON YOUNG MAN as he settles himself into a pew,
　　　　ceremoniously places a white pill in front of him, and looks up
　　　　smiling .

#### YOUNG MAN
**Father,-we're all yours...**

#### DISSOLVE:

---

197.　　*INT JAIL MORGUE. Showing a body lying on a slab, covered
　　　　by a sheet. There is, O.S., the SOUND of a woman bitterly
　　　　sobbing softly. PULL BACK to disclose Nicholas standing there,
　　　　together with an older couple; the woman cries, the man, fierce-
　　　　eyed, his face frozen in hostility and grief. Nicholas makes a
　　　　gesture towards them, then turns, starts to walk out.*

198.　　INT.JAIL CORRIDOR- MOVING- on Nicholas, treading wearily,
　　　　staring straight ahead. There are O.S. SHOUTS from cells on
　　　　both sides.

<u>INMATES (v.o.)</u>
"Hey, Father, I want to talk to you about my immortal soul ..."

"Quit bugging him, Leroy.
Fruits don't go to heaven, you know that. ..

"What a friend I have in Jesus
All my grieves and joys to share..."

"Hey, Father- is it true, when the Pope takes
a leak he keeps his eyes closed?"


199.   *INT. BRIGHTLY LIT CENTRAL OFFICE of this Police Division.*
       *On Helen, seated in a chair, waiting. She suddenly springs to*
       *her feet; Nicholas comes up to her.*

NICHOLAS
(*astonished*)
I thought you were staying -- ?


<u>HELEN</u>
I changed my mind!
(*taking his arm, moving him along*)
Come on,...

<u>DISSOLVE:</u>

---

200.  Cont.
<u>NICHOLAS</u>
...anyone could see from that intergalactic look, he must have
escaped from somewhere! But the cops took the position they
had to protect <u>me</u> from him!

So the minute he saw those uniforms -
(*makes a motion, popping a pill into his mouth*)
Strychnine! God knows where he got the stuff. His face
simply decomposed. 100 years in ten seconds. And never
stopped grinning  once...

...not that I didn't preach—My God, I spewed out my trunkful of
reliable suicide stand-bys ----Jaspers, Buber, Tillich, the whole

87

Galaxy---and struck out on each one. Then I suddenly remembered my father's brother, Uncle Max, --who was an artilleryman in WW2, His unit happened to have helped liberate a Nazi death camp and he described a strange scene he once came upon: just freed prisoners—themselves starving skeletons in filthy striped pajamas, ---helping one another to climb up on an empty ammunition box so each could jump down on the barely breathing body of a man in an S.S. Guard uniform who was taking too long(for them) to die...

(another tone)
Max told about how some US Chaplain by sheer chance wandered onto the proceedings and after a few minutes tried to stop what was going on since the Nazi was barely breathing by then anyway, ) But the filthy striped pajamas turned on *him!* , shouting *"habst nich das recht"* (you don't have the right--!) --In a kind of maniacal tone, which some skeletal pajama told Max meant: shut up, shut up, what the hell do you know about it anyway ....!

(*shaking his head*)
Revenge! It's a contagion ! You can see it everywhere - the kid with his pills showed it on his face. His parents, too. In fact, you can see it every day, on the street. And I suddenly realized: it's the same look I keep trying to challenge my congregation with in sermons week after week.
Sermons they're now trying to fire me for!

\*\*\*\*\*\*

*She reaches across, and takes his hand in both of hers. A moment of intimacy, ineffable, excruciating.*

DISSOLVE:

_____

Ext Sidewalk—Moving on Helen and Nicholas. She has her arm linked through his and is talking briskly, trying to make plans

**Helen**
I'll tell you what we'll do, Nicko, dear...
(*she thinks, organizing*)

We'll go home, rent a car—mine seems to have sort of
developed a death rattle in the groin—and tomorrow we'll drive
straight South across the border to Las Fuentes
(Looking at him, a note of entreaty)
People always go to the hot countries to recover, don't
they? I mean, where he weather's warm—you know—where the
natives ae friendly... No phones. No angst. No apocalypse talk, no
existential this and that. If you don't want to, we won't even talk.. - I
haven't really listened to silence in years. And we won't wear
clothes. We can even try out the ninety-seven and a half different
positions -we've never had time to ---


NICHOLAS
(stepping on the street, raising a finger)
Taxi!

A taxi pulls up. Nicholas puts Helen inside, then closes the door,
remaining himself on the sidewalk. She looks her question through the
open window.

NICHOLAS
Anyone calls -the Bishop, newspaper people, - tell Louise to deflect
them. You haven't seen me, you don't know where I am. If I'm not
home by morning I'll leave a message...


HELEN
Why? ...

NICHOLAS
I have to give a deposition. Besides,
the kids' parents are still there.

HELEN
But they don't want anything from -

NICHOLAS
Me. Not them. I want something!
(a pause, Speaking rather matter- of-fact)
Not that there's much of a chance. But they might- problematic or
not- help me find whether I've still got a vocation or not...

He turns and moves O.S.; CAMERA Tremulous, eyes moist with tears.

**HELEN**
Nicko...

*(HOLDING on Helen)*


DISSOLVE:

---

201.   *INT. AIRPORT WAITING ROOM, on Nicholas and Helen-Nicholas saying goodbye. This, of course, is the same scene we have already seen twice before. Nicholas bends and kisses Helen goodbye.*

**NICHOLAS (v.o.)**
**"Blessed sister, Holy Mother..."**

DISSOLVE:

---

202.   EXT. A FOUNTAIN IN A RELIGIOUS RETREAT- DAY. Open to all sects. Like the one in Tasa Hara in Carmel Valley, or on the Big Sur highway past Big Sur. Nicholas is strolling by, dressed in work clothes, very primitively, garden implements in hand; obviously very absorbed within himself.

**NICHOLAS (v.o.)**
**"Spirit of the fountain spirit of the garden ..."**

DISSOLVE:

---

203.   FIELD NEARBY. Nicholas is working the ground; he works hard, he sweats in the sun, obviously he is not used to it.

204.   Cont.

**NICHOLAS (v.o.)**
**"Suffer us not to mock ourselves with falsehood..."**
*Nicholas stands up, stares.*

205. ANOTHER PART OF THE FIELD. Fleeting illusion of the
Japanese man we saw earlier, the disfigured victim of the bomb
blast at Hiroshima, appears preposterously for a second,
silently lecturing, then vanishes.

206.

DISSOLVE:

---

207. *EXT. WOOD PILE. Nicholas is chopping wood.*

**NICHOLAS (v.o.)**
**"Teach us to care..."**

*He suddenly stops, peering intently.*

208. REVERSE ANGLE. WOOD PILE - what he sees: the covered
body on the slab in the morgue, in the middle of the wood pile.
It slowly vanishes.

DISSOLVE:

---

209. *GRAVELLED PATH OF A TREE. Nicholas slowly walking,
hands clasped behind him, sunk in thought.*

**NICHOLAS (v.o.)**
**"...and not to care..."**

As we watch, the scene becomes Nicholas as he trod the jail corridor,
caught in a hail of jeers between the O.S. cells; the epithets bludgeoning
like actual blows...

DISSOLVE:

---

210. INT. BARREN,AUSTERE  DINING HALL, deserted, except for
Nicholas, alone at a table with a book. Trying to read.

**NICHOLAS (v.o.)**
**"...teach us to sit still..."**

*As Nicholas suddenly looks up from his book. He HEARS a very very faint SOUND, inexplicable- it might be a distant car on a road somewhere- it lasts only for a fleeting instant, puzzling, then vanishes. He returns to his book.*

<u>DISSOLVE</u>:

---

211.    EXT. ROCKY GROUND. NIGHT. Nicholas preparing to sleep on the rocks, with only a blanket and no pillow.

<u>**NICHOLAS (v.o.)**</u>
**"...and even among these rocks..."**

*Nicholas closes his eyes, pulls the blanket over him, CAMERA HOLDING STEADY.*

<u>**NICHOLAS (v.o.)**</u>
**"...Sister, Mother..."**

<u>DISSOLVE</u>:

---

212.    ON Nicholas, sleeping, late at night. CAMERA MOVES TO HIS FACE- CLOSE UP- it seems to be undergoing something- perhaps some sort of nightmare.

213.    SERIES OF KALEIDOSCOPIC IMAGES, blurred. Helen sitting down on Nicholas' lap in his study; Helen taking the speck out of his eye on the bathtub ledge; Helen gesticulating, enthusiastically showing him the Yoga exercise in the bedroom; Helen waiting for him in the police station; Helen looking after him through the open window in the cab...these are very swift and blurred, perhaps soft focus...

<u>**NICHOLAS (v.o.)**</u>
**"...spirit of the sea..."**

Here we begin distinctly to hear the SOUND, of an automobile engine; a car speeding along a road somewhere. The noise of this engine will increase in tempo until the end of this sequence.

## NICHOLAS (v.o.)
### "...suffer me not to be separated ..."

*Nicholas suddenly wakes up, awash with sweat, bolt upright. His eyes
wide open. He apparently has had a nightmare vision of some horrific
happening. His head seems plagued by the SOUND of an engine, a
terrible sound he can't shake off.*

*He gets up, starts to walk woodenly across the little court, CAMERA
HOLDING on him. He comes to a courtyard. Everything glossed with
moonlight. He seems to move faster and faster, though somnambulistic
ally. It's as if he was in the grip of a sudden, very terrible premonition.
He unlocks a shed.*

214.    *INT. SHED, as Nicholas comes into it. Walks through and exits
        the other side.*

215.    *EXT. LITTLE UTILITY SHED, as Nicholas comes up there,
        fiddles with the latch, opens the door, switches on the light.*
        (NOTE:  The O.S. SOUND of the automobile is now
        preposterously and excruciatingly LOUD).

216.    INT. SHACK. A phone all by itself on a little wooden table. As
        we look at it, it begins- suddenly- crushingly- electrifyingly- to
        RING.

CLOSE IN on this phone, all by itself.  Blended with this RINGING, as it
were, is a SOUND superimposition -the by now recognizable sound of
that indelible sickening CRASH, first heard in the prologue and then in
the second section . The phone suddenly melds into image of the
broken clock on the truck dash, its glass shattered, its hands arrested at
five minutes to twelve. FREEZE FRAME. Seconds of utter silence.

# PIECES

"PORTENTS FAVORABLE FOR LUCK TO CHANGE;
ACCEPT FAVORS GRACEFULLY. SOMEONE YOU
KNOW MAY GIVE YOU A PRICELESS GIFT..."

DISSOLVE:

---

EXT. PLAYYARD SUBURBAN HOUSE- DAY. On Ro. He is standing there, accepting something being handed to him from below: a broken rag doll- half of a child's comb - bits of lettuce- several ripped pages from picture magazines - his expression is very complicated - a sort of determined smile, but the sorrow shows through.

**ATTENDANT (v.o.)**
**Aha!  You see?...**

*CAMERA TILTS DOWN, losing Ro, and we are looking at a baby in a basket.  A GIRL about 4 years old, with big eyes and a floppy head of the Mongoloid child.  She doesn't speak, continually burbles, and keeps handing stuff up to Ro, out of CAMERA.*

**ATTENDANT (v.o.)**
**Oh, she definitely recognizes you! I mean, we don't give our precious things away to just anybody, do we dear?**

217.     ANOTHER ANGLE. On Ro and PAULINE. Pauline: a tense, dark, still very lovely- though obviously ravaged - woman of around Ro' age. Standing next to him, obviously invested in the scene, she is Ro's ex- wife.

**ATTENDANT (v.o.)**
**No sir, we certainly don't. Only that's my mommy and daddy - *that's* who that is!  Yes sir! My mommy and daddy who came to take me out on my birthday!**

218.     On baby in the basket, grinning, tearing pages from
          a picture book.

**ATTENDANT (v.o.)**
**Doctor says from the way she holds her head up and all, she's probably on the upper end of the watchamacallit scale, - you know, what they use to measure them by.  I mean, maybe not even a true Mongoloid at all...**

219.    On Ro and Pauline. As they reach down, each carrying an end
        of the basket- it's really like a laundry basket - and start off
        carrying their retarded child between them; they have done this
        many times before.

219. Cont.

ATTENDANT (v.o.)
Say goodbye to Karen now, children!
Happy returns, have a nice birthday...


CHORUS OF CHILDREN
(voices over)
Good- bye...Ka-ren!...

DISSOLVE:

---

220.    EXT. SIDEWALK- A KIND OF CROWDED, CLUTTERY, TICK-
        TACKY BUSINESS DISTRICT.  On Ro and Pauline, lugging the
        baby in the basket between them. (NOTE: the area is perhaps
        vaguely like Santa Monica Boulevard, with its "photographic
        parlors," film sex shows, etc).

PAULINE (v.o.)
I'm sure I could swing it...

221.    STREET INTERSECTION.  As Ro and Pauline start to cross
        the street.

PAULINE (v.o.)
If I could get a woman in to help...

222.    CLOSE on baby in basket, being joggled along through traffic.

RO (v.o.)
Who'd pay?

223.    OPPOSITE SIDEWALK, as Ro and Pauline step up to the
        pavement, turn right, and continue walking, the baby still
        between them, of course.

#### PAULINE (v.o.)
#### All right.  Borrow the money, then...

224.   INT. FIRST FLOOR HALLWAY OF RAMSHACKLE BUSINESS
       BUILDING.  As Pauline and Ro turn in, still toting the baby
       between them.

#### PAULINE (v.o.)
#### I mean, she'd be better off than with old Mother Macree...

225.   On baby being carried up a flight of old stairs,
       which go CREAK, CREAK.

225.  Cont.

#### RO (v.o.)
**...who treats her as sort of a heavenly credit card, licensed by the welfare department? Redeemable in blessings galore in the form of substantial check each month?  Besides- it's the only place in the world the "baby" -- apologize- "relates to" anymore...**

226.   SECOND FLOOR HALLWAY -INT.-on Ro and Pauline as they
       are walking down past various sleazy glass office doors. There
       are photographic salons, fly-by-night record companies, etc.

#### PAULINE (v.o.)
#### If I could have her with me for just a few months...?

#### RO (v.o.)
**...you'd develop shingles, your sex life would go smash, our telephone bills would go way up. And Karen would pine for the anesthetic bliss of Mrs. Morrison's Mongoloid menagerie...**

227.   INT. ANTEROOM OFFICE. As Ro and Pauline enter carrying
       the baby. There are pictures on the wall of naked models, a
       glass partition, waiting desks, and stills from various more or
       less mildly pornographic movies. There is the SOUND O.S. of
       harsh rock and roll playing somewhere.  Pauline snatches the
       baby up for a second in her arms, from the basket, cuddling
       her.

#### PAULINE (v.o.)
#### Not Mongoloid! You heard what the doctor said. Upper Level...

#### RO
*(sympathetically)*

**Sure. Upper level...**
**A MAN comes out from behind the partition. Youngish, plump, a
cigar in his mouth, a green eye-shade on his head, a pencil behind
his ear, and a sheaf of papers in one hand.**

### MAN
*(to Pauline)*
**Mrs. Williams? Audition, one o'clock?**

*At this, Pauline kisses the baby, puts her back in the basket, disappears
behind a partition with the man. Ro sits down, takes a book out, settles
himself on the waiting bench, studies. Baby gurgles away.*

### DISSOLVE:

---

227.    CLOSE on baby in the basket, playing with some pictures
        someone gave her. MUSIC, rock and loud, still playing O.S.
        Two girls are talking nearby.

### FIRST GIRL (v.o.)
**Camus was a fink plain and simple. Anybody who can
sentimentalize Camus- my God, the man never even openly
denounced the Algerie Francaise movement -**

### SECOND GIRL (v.o.)
**Look: anyone who can say Camus was a fink suffers from that
boring absolutist Either-Or-Syndrome. Which, your dear buddy
Sartre exemplifies, incidentally...**

228.    ON nearby bench, showing the two GIRLS who have been
        doing the talking. Very sexy, and yet, at the same time,
        obviously intelligent. Intellectual hookers.

### FIRST GIRL
**Don't call him my buddy! I don't necessarily defend Sartre just
because I can't stand Camus!**

### SECOND GIRL
**Who told me last week? Great man! Refused a Nobel Prize!**

### FIRST GIRL
**Did Camus refuse it? You bet your ass he didn't!**

99

## SECOND GIRL
**Proving what, may I ask?**

## FIRST GIRL
**Proving- when it comes to moral courage- really
making an out-cry-**

At this point there is a SOUND of a baby beginning to cry.
Perhaps after a fall.


229.     *MEDIUM ON ANTEROOM. As Pauline comes out half
         undressed, a "script" under one arm, and grabs up the
         baby in her arms, comforting her. Everyone stares.*

### DISSOLVE:

---

230.     INT. RESTAURANT- TABLE- not an expensive place, perhaps
a        place popular with children. ON Pauline and Ro, reading aloud
         from her "script" and laughing. Their heads are close together.
         Baby is sleeping in the basket nearby on the floor.

## RO
*(quoting from script)*
**"How about a few feet of skin?"**

## PAULINE
**"Cheaper by the ton, tiger. If you think you've got the reach!"**

## RO
**"Directions: he chases her naked around the pool. They both
jump in. They are joined by two huge guppie fish..."**
**(incredulous, looking up)**
**What?**

## PAULINE
**Guppies are very sexy. You know, big mouths. Anyway, this
outfit specializes in marine porn. I mean, under water every scene
takes longer to happen. Right?**

## RO
**Seven times in three pages? C'mon!**

### PAULINE

That's why they have to keep recruiting all the time.
*(closing the script)*
Nothing uses up talent like porn believe me.
*(more intimate tone)*
Anyway, these days I'm chaste myself.  Can't you tell by my
complexion?   I go on reading binges.
Right now, Checkov, an old addiction.
*(smiling)*
*(continued)*

231. Cont.

### PAULINE

*(continued)*
You'd be surprised how soothing it is. I mean, I come home from
that progressive, pardon- re-vo-lu-tionar-y- nursery school, where
the poor little bastards are already so politicalized, they run around
all day playing end-of-the-world games! Guevarra this! Mao that!
Boom, Bang, off with their heads!...
*(sighing)*
Believe me, I'm glad to climb into bed with a peeled apple.
Sighing over whether Ivan Ilyitch is ever going to climb out of
that goddam ravine!...

### WAITER (v.o.)
Excuse me...

CAMERA PULLS BACK to disclose a WAITER standing there with a
birthday cake, four candles brightly lit, burning.

### WAITER
Did someone order a cake...?

### PAULINE
Yes!
*(looking defiantly at Ro)*

### WAITER
*(clearing his throat, singing)*
"Happy birthday to you

Happy birthday to you Happy birthday dear--"
*(he is at a loss, the name escapes him)*

101

**PAULINE**
Karen!


**WAITER**
"...Karen...
Happy birthday to youuuu!"


231.   *Cont. The baby never wakes up.  Ro shakes his head, bemused.
The waiter places the cake on the table .*


DISSOLVE:

---

232.   *INT. PARKED CAR- DUSK.  On Ro and Pauline; car is parked
on the coastal highway, getting the last of the view.  Ro is
looking through a series of photographs which Pauline is
handing him.*


**PAULINE**

**This guys was sort of an idiot, of course. Spastic, but with
flair. He told me he was writing a novel to be read by touch,
only then he got on to films, aleatory films ...**

233.   ON Pauline- CLOSE UP- a study, losing Ro here.

**PAULINE**
**The idea was you were supposed to pick out a film strip from a fish
bowl as you went in, and afterwards it was pasted together.  Lots of
lectures on the *Scissors as The Central Symbol of Art in Our Time*
or something** ...

**RO (v.o.)**
**My God, who's that?**

**PAULINE**
**Don't you remember my sister Libby?...**
*(chattily)*
**Big wheel in Women's Lib.
"OL-MSCB:  OFF LIMITS- MALE SEX CHAUVINIST BASTARDS!"**
*(rueful)*
**She's been trying to turn me on to the auto-erotic thing.  How when**

you do it alone, it's not only "political," but better, lasts longer. Like one of those long-playing moon things...
(*sardonic sigh*)
But I'm hopeless, I still like to have somebody helping...


234.     ON A PHOTOGRAPH.  Showing Ro and Pauline. As they were perhaps a few years ago, standing arm-in- arm on a bridge, in a foreign country.


234.   Cont.

### RO (v.o.)
My God, there's a silly looking pair...
obviously never going anywhere .

### PAULINE (v.o.)
(*looking herself*)
The man looks like a regular census taker. The way he's got his ear- if you'll forgive the expression - cocked?

### RO (v.o.)
And look at the woman's mouth!  Wide open.
Ready to gobble up everything in sight.

235.     ON the two of them, in the car, gazing at the photograph.

### PAULINE
Trying to get in one word to his five, no doubt...

### RO
As long as it's the last word, right?

### PAULINE
(*suddenly grabbing up the photograph and tearing it to pieces:  the weight of the past has suddenly slipped into the banter*)
As you said; they're never going anywhere!

*She puts the car into gear, drives suddenly off.*

### DISSOLVE:

---

236.     EXT. RO'S TREE HOUSE- NIGHT. On parked car. Pauline is
         seated inside, head leaning out the window. As Ro comes up to
         her with an arm full of vegetables, dumps them into the front
         seat.

**RO**
**Vitamin A.  Marvelous with Chekov.**
**How about some more? Carrots?  Lettuce?**

236.  Cont.

**PAULINE**
(*shakes her head*)
**No.**

**RO**
**It's all going to be bull-dozed in a few days anyway. New road, new**
**power plant. And new- naturally- demonstration...**
(*he notices she's trembling*)
**Hey, what's happening...**

**PAULINE**
**Just my lousy cardiovascular system, that's all.**
**I got a very lousy cardiovascular system.**

*Ro opens the door, so she can get out.*

**PAULINE**
(*continued*)
**I forgot where, but I read a story recently. A kid walks around, and**
**like, everything keeps receding, evaporating, becoming harder to**
**get hold of...**
(*her voice gets more and more tense*)
**I mean, he's strangling sort of, inside let's say a portable hurricane**
**or something, and there are lots of scenes, a whole bunch of odd**
**stuff happening , two feet away. Only where he is - at the center-**
**nothing - He might as well be stoned out of his ever loving mind of**
**course! The son of a bitch doesn't appreciate it. What he really**
**craves is to be tossed around, play dress-up , get smashed to**
**pieces like everybody else...**
(*very close to tears*)
**Actually, it was stupid,  I mean, I don't really**
**know why I even bring the boring thing up...**

*She stands there. Tears well up in her eyes suddenly, bereft. He takes her in his arms- an old tenderness triggered off- in comfort. HOLD.*

DISSOLVE:

---

237.    TOP OF REDWOOD TREE. ON Ro, rather CLOSE ANGLE. He is sitting there, in the Yoga position, calm, as he was earlier. SOUND O.S. of students chanting: *"Nous sommes tous des juifs allemands!"*

### RO (v.o.)
**They tell me I was very photogenic,-**
**through a telescopic lens, of course!...**

238.    Student seen earlier, on TV, with a sash labeled "DEAN." Talking "earnestly" into a mike.

### RO (v.o.)
**As demonstrations go, though, it was tame. Probably because everybody had trains and planes to catch...**

239.    ON Ro again, up on the treetop. SOUND NOW O.S. of the chain saws, fugal with the students chanting.

### RO (v.o.)
**Though I had to come down a little earlier than planned...**

240.    ON a young black cat, crouched in the middle of tree branches, scared to go up or down.

### RO (v.o.)
**...for humanitarian reasons...**

*Ro comes INTO SCENE, grabs cat gently, cradles it in his arms, and swings over to another tree branch on his way down.*

### RO (v.o.)
**...and by a rather indirect route...**

DISSOLVE:

---

241.     INT. CAR ON HIGHWAY, SOUTHERN CALIFORNIA
        LANDSCAPE NOW, still the coastal road. MEDIUM CLOSE on
        a BOY, holding the black cat on his lap that we have seen
        earlier, together with a little portable Sony tape recorder-
        recognizable as Ro's. The child wears glasses, is relentlessly
        articulate, and has, alas, certain monster-like aspects; in other
        words, a typical future whacked-out Jewish intellectual. He is
        about 9 years old.


241. Cont.

**BOY**
(*reciting into the recorder*)
**My name is Marvin Charles Goldberg!**
**Nine years old. I'm going to San Diego...**
(*handing the instrument to someone O.S.*)

**RO (v.o.)**
**Now you?...**

**My name is Rowen Williams . Thirty years old.**
**Going to Santa Fe, to see some Sand Paintings...**

*We wait. There is the SOUND of the tape being slightly rewound,*
*stopped , turned back again. The boy watches all this intently.*

**RECORDER**
**"...going to Santa Fee to see some Sand Paintings..."**

**BOY**
**Hey?  Neat!**
(thinks)
**My favorite flavor is strawberry. My favorite comic is The Hulk.**
**My favorite star is -**

**FATHER (v.o.)**
**Never mind that stuff. Give him some statistics!**
(*pause, to Ro*)
**Kid's got a terrific memory for statistics.  Wait'll you hear-**

**MOTHER (v.o.)**
**Albert, please...**

**FATHER (v.o.)**
**Go on, Marvin. Tell us about the G.N.P.**

241.  Cont.

**BOY**
(*triggered*)
**The G.N.P.**

(*clears his throat*)
**Last year the Gross National Product of the United States...**

242.  ROADSIDE- PAN SWEEP, as from perhaps a moving car, along the roadway edge: series of billboards, the first one for a soap deodorant, showing a happy pair frolicking. Title- "Don't You Wish Everybody Did."

**BOY (v.o.)**
**...was nine hundred...**

Billboard, cigarette ad, showing a scoreboard of tar residues, by percentages. Caption- **"The Filter Makes The Difference."**

**BOY (v.o.)**
**...twenty-five hundred thousand ...**

Billboard, liquor ad. Caption- **"Only The Very Best."** Another billboard. Brassiere ad. Woman blowing a leaf off her hand, just in bra and panties. Caption- **"Lighter Than A Feather."**

**BOY (v.o.)**
**...million dollars ...**

243.  INT. CAR, centering on child.  He has finished his stint. Very soberly awaiting the next challenge .

**FATHER (v.o.)**
**See?  Ask him anything!**
(*thinking*)
**How about automobiles?**

**BOY**
**Automobiles!**
(*slight reflection*)
**The total number of...**

244.    ANOTHER SLOW PAN on portion of the moving highway. Several flares placed in the middle of the road- warning flares which the highway police sometimes put up.

244. Cont.

**BOY (v.o.)**
**...passenger cars produced...**

*Cops directing traffic by a hang up ahead .*

**BOY (v.o.)**
**...last year in the whole country was ...**

Bits and pieces of a wrecked automobile strewn along the highway.

**BOY (v.o.)**
**....eight million ...**

More and more pieces of wreckage. Blinking police car. The dense ganglia of a highway accident.

**BOY (v.o.)**
**...eight hundred and forty-eight thousand ...**

On highway:  the other end of the accident- perhaps an ambulance, and then the other set of flares.

**BOY (v.o.)**
**...six hundred and twenty!**

Billboard- "**What Can You Do?  Write Citizens For Cleaner Environment, Incorporated. 223 West Third Street. Washington, D. C.**"

**FATHER (v.o.)**
**See?  Go on, The state of California?**

Series of placards by the roadside, like Mennen ads. They are advertising a huge, imminent, under- construction tract.

First one reads- "**Belleview Estates.**"

BOY (v.o.)
California, By 1975 the population of California ...

Placard- **"Three and Four Bedrooms."**

BOY (v.o.)
**...will amount to...**

Placard- **"All Electric Kitchens."**

244. Cont.
BOY (v.o.)
**...twenty-two million ...**

Placard- **"Utilities  Underground!"**

BOY (v.o.)
**...two hundred and...**

Placard- **"Vets: No Down. Others : Easy Terms."**

BOY (v.o.)
**...twenty-four thousand ...**

*On roadside. We are passing part of the half-built tract now, already partly occupied. It is what you might expect. The new prefabricated slums. Kids, people bulging behind big redwood fence, and all the other paraphernalia full on exhibit of rising material expectations, materialized.*

BOY (v.o.)
**...making it number one, nationwide...**

Roadside stone, whitewashed rock- **"Repent Ye Sinners!"**

BOY (v.o.)
**Missiles!**
(*clears his throat*)
**The Atlas ICBM...**

*Roadside group of sullen Negroes, around a parked car. They stare, their hostility is palpable.*

BOY (v.o.)
**...with a range of six thousand miles...**

Billboard -white man, seated with two boys, one black, in baseball bleachers, all three with popcorn bags. Caption- "**Big Brothers, Inc. For Those Who Care To Help.**"

**BOY (v.o.)**
**...has a thrust of three hundred and sixty thousand pounds...**

Nuclear Reactor Plant. It says- "**Danger: Authorized Personnel Only.**" A plant like the one, perhaps, at San Clemente, California.

244.   Cont.

**BOY (v.o.)**
**...on the other hand, the Titan can go seven thousand miles...**

Beach front sign: "**Danger.  Beach Contaminated.**"

**BOY (v.o.)**
**...from a thrust of only three hundred and...**

*A bunch of skin divers, hippies, have just come out of the water. They wave, very friendly .*

**BOY (v.o.)**
**...forty thousand pounds...**

**FATHER (v.o.)**
**Okay, Marvin, fine.  He gets the idea...**

**BOY (v.o.)**
(*relentless*)
**...as for the Polaris A Three- equipped with MRVs- Multiple-Re-entry-Vehicles  - ...**

*We are now passing a travelling Water Color Society. They are seated, painting the scene, the contaminated ocean looks very blue, of course, on the easels.*

**MOTHER (v.o.)**
(*plaintive*)
**I told you, Max, not to -**

**BOY (v.o.)**
**...it can go twenty-five hundred miles...**

**FATHER (v.o.)**
I said knock it off!- didn't you hear me?

**BOY (v.o.)**
...with a thrust of...

**FATHER (v.o.)**
(*explosive*)
Knock it off, you little creep!
Or I swear, I'll have to stuff a cork in your mouth!

245.    EXT. ROADSIDE on a woman standing by a stalled or stuck
        car. She is holding a hand-made sign up to passing cars, and
        has a rueful smile. CAMERA ZOOMS up to her. We see it
        is...Helen! Her sign reads: "**Dumb Female Trick- Out Of Gas.
        Sir Galahad, Where Are You?**"

DISSOLVE:

---

246.    INT. FRONT SEAT GREEN MUSTANG.  Helen and Ro seated
side    by side, the cat on Ro's lap, the tape recorder between them. They
        are driving down the highway together.

**TAPE RECORDER**
(*of Father's voice*)
"I said knock it off- didn't you hear me?"
(*of boy's voice*)
"with a thrust of..."
(*of Father's voice*)
"Knock it off you creep.  Or I'll stuff a cork in your mouth!"

The recorder is shut off. Helen and Ro are laughing.
CLOSE ON Helen, losing Ro.

**RO (v.o.)**
I'd forgotten what a wonderful laugh the woman had. Only since I'd
seen her- only a few weeks -something seemed to have...
immobilized her eyes...

247.    CLOSE ON Ro. Sitting, looking at the roadside, holding the cat.

**RO (v.o.)**

She couldn't seem to stop talking, either. Acting the stranger. Oozing
all those "Confessions" strangers seem to reserve for one another.

DISSOLVE:

---

248.    *INT. CAR. Helen, talking away animatedly as she drives.*

**RO (v.o.)**

I learned her daughter, 19 years old, an airline stewardess.
Flies two times a week from New York to Tokyo.
Wasn't that absurd work for a grown woman?

DISSOLVE:

---

249.    ROADSIDE JUICE STAND. ON Helen, still talking, drinking juice.

**RO (v.o.)**

Her great-aunt- whom she was going to visit- lives in some place
called Cahone, Colorado. The elevation is higher than the population...

DISSOLVE:

---

250.    MOVING- SPARSE ROADSIDE TERRAIN. We are now definitely
       in more tropical territory.

**RO (v.o.)**

Her linguistic preference?  Spanish over French. French was
marvelous- for instance, the word for blood, sang- very elegant.

251.    *INT. CAR. Helen, driving, still talking away,*
       *illustrating with her hands.*

RO (v.o.)
But Spanish? Sangre! You could taste it!

DISSOLVE:

---

252.  INT. FRONT SEAT OF CAR.  On Ro and Helen.  Both much
      more casual, Ro's jacket unbuttoned in the heat, Helen leaning
      back, silent, smiling. She seems to be thinking of something.

RO (v.o.)
After awhile, though, she began to relax...

HELEN
Every other line- okay?

*Ro nods "yes".*

HELEN
(*continuing*)
"I chased a health nut up a tree..."

252.  Cont.

RO
(*mock outrage*)
"My God, is she speaking of me?"

HELEN
"He had women: a slew..."

RO
"That's a lie! Just a few!..."

HELEN
"But they sawed him to size..."

RO
"-on TV!"

*They look at each other, both laughing.*

---

253.    INT. MUSTANG- on Ro and Helen. Very late afternoon,
approaching dusk. We are now definitely in Arizona desert
country... Ro is examining a map open on his lap.

## RO
**According to the map, there's a crossroads
ahead, you can turn off ...**

## HELEN
**I'd take you through. But the thought of going through
the desert a night - ?**

## RO
*(folding up the map)*
**No problem.   I'll get a ride...**
*(looking at the cat, which has snuggled up to Helen)*
**Hey...maybe I thought to leave you "Finney?"
Since he's definitely showing a preference...**

## HELEN
**"Finney?"**

253. Cont.

## RO
**After "Finnegan's Wake" Honor of James Joyce ... I read, you
know, where Joyce said what a writer needed was Silence, Exile,
and Cunning. But if you ask me, what he really was describing was
our friend Finney here -**
*(stroking the cat)*
**isn't that right, mister?**

**That cat goes MEOW, loud.**

254.    *BARREN DESERT CROSSROADS , four directional signs. A
fantastic OLD LADY is revealed, kneeling on the ground, her ear to the
earth. She gets up, grinning , a fantastic sight. A seamed face ,great
age, high- button shoes, an old-fashioned hat. She listens - a car is
definitely approaching. The old lady is carrying a little bag of belongings,
a homespun staff, a shovel, her beautiful head glinting in the setting
sun. She waits. The green mustang pulls up to the crossroads and
stops. She immediately- even peremptorily - marches over to it, smiling.*

114

### OLD LADY
**Took you a few seconds longer than I figured...**
*(handing her bag inside, without further ado)*
**Help me with this, would you young fellow?**

*She opens the door, and settles herself in the back .*


255.     *INT. CAR.  As the old lady gets in.*
         *Ro and Helen staring at each other.*

### OLD LADY
**Only goin' fifteen miles or so.**
**But I want to get there before dark.**
*(a thought)*
**You were goin' south, weren't you?...**


### RO
*(delicately)*
**As a matter of fact...**

*Helen has already started up the car, and heads straight ahead; her action answers the question. He looks at her; old lady settles back, smiling.*


256.     INT. MUSTANG. ON all three.
         The car is humming along. It is now quite dark .

### OLD LADY
*(to Helen)*
**Striking the way he favors you- Your son, I mean...**
**They don't answer.  She goes on.**

### OLD LADY
*(continuing)*
**My own son, God forgive me- one of the ugliest creatures God ever made. And damn fool to boot!**
*(suppressed mirth)*
**Last week the idiot tried to inter me in one of those senile mausoleums - you know, - if you need something, they plug you in... Breathing machines, eating machines, even peeing machines**
...

115

---

257. CLOSE- on old lady alone. Showing her really remarkable face.

### OLD LADY
Told him, no thanks , I'll do my own peein', long's I'm able...
(proudly)
I'm ninety-three years old. Been comin' to the desert forty
years. You can look me up in any library:
Alma Peterson: "Desert Flora Of The Southwest"...

258. INT. CAR. ON all three. As Ro reaches for his knapsack.

### RO
(to Helen, ironic)
**Mother dear!** Isn't it getting' to be snack time - ?

258. Cont.

### OLD LADY
Not for me ,thanks just the same. I'm done with all that hard labor,
thank God. I mean, eating, digesting, the rest of it. My age, you just
have to keep callin' the roll.
(mock stern)

### OLD LADY
(continued)

Kidneys? Liver?
What tricks you wrecks planning to pull on me today?
(silent mirth again)
A funny subject for sure only as the fellow says:
I'm through laughing ...

DISSOLVE:

---

259. INT. CAR, deep into the desert. It is now nearly dark- the sun a
vermillion smudge on the horizon. A wind has come up.

#### OLD LADY
**Don't you hear it?**
*(she listens)*
**Water running in veins all around hereabouts.**
**When I was young, my hearing was so keen, -**
*(suddenly straightening up- to Helen)*
**Excuse me, ma'am, right here's the place.**

**She takes her belongings, her staff, her shovel.**
**Prepares to get out.**

#### RO
**Going to do a little seed gathering, Mrs. Peterson?**

260.    EXT. CAR, as old lady gets out, and stands there for a second: all three are in CAMERA VIEW.

#### OLD LADY
**Hell no!  Just want to return a little of what belongs to the area, that's all.  Includin' myself, of course.**
*(has a thought, removes her wristwatch, handing it in)*
**Here. Cheap. But still runs. You might as well have it.**

*She notices them staring at her, especially Ro. She smiles.*

#### OLD LADY
*(to Helen)*
**What's he lookin' so woebegone about!**
*(to Ro, patient)*
**Think of what I've used up getting to be this decrepit, boy-**
**I mean, plants, animals, whatnot. Don't you think I'm obliged to give something back.**
*(reflects)*
**Navahos have a song -**
**not that anyone can translate Navaho, of course ...**
*(she thinks, then speaks softly)*
**"Fashion a hole, heap up a mound**
**Turn back to seed, welcome the ground ...**

**Whoever comes by, let him scatter these stones**
**Hallow the sky, make good use of my bones..."**

*She smiles at them, turns, trudges off into the desert.*

260.    ON Ro and Helen - CLOSE. Staring after her.

261.    LONG ANGLE.  ON the back of the old lady, slowly evaporating
        into the desert landscape.

DISSOLVE:

---

262.    EXT. DESERT- NIGHT. It is cold. The stars are out. ON Ro-
        sitting alone, concentrating, in his habitual nightly meditative
        position, the Lotus.

**HELEN (v.o.)**
**I'm cold...**
(*rather roguish*)
**Aren't you cold, Finney?...**

263.    ON Helen: curled up on the ground, in Ro's sleeping bag, the
        cat close to her.

**HELEN**
(*shaking her head*)
**We're not getting through, "Fin-"-.**
**No communication at all-- .**
(*deliberately*)
**Maybe if we put it in rhyme?...**

264.    Ro. Seated calmly, gazing at the distant sky.

265. Cont.
**HELEN (v.o.)**
**"Night is in the desert is cold, if you want to be**
**warm, then be bold."**

266. Sleeping bag:  it's empty.

**HELEN (v.o.)**
(*chattering a little*)
**"Whereupon she froze and threw off all her clothes..."**

267.    ON Ro. He looks up. What he sees, of course, is a revelation.
        He gets up, comes TOWARD CAMERA and O.S.

**HELEN (v.o.)**
**"The results were just like she'd foretold!"**

*INTO SHOT where Ro had been comes Finney, the cat. It stares: opens its mouth, whines softly.*

DISSOLVE:

---

268.    DESERT ROAD- EARLY SUNRISE. On Finnegan, the cat- it runs across the highway, underneath wheels of a huge truck, passing, going east.

**RO (v.o.)**
**Finnegan!**

And now Ro COMES INTO SCENE. For a second it's not clear what happened- then the cat is shown unscathed, on the road, the ECHOES of the truck dying away. Ro picks up the animal.

**RO**
**What's the matter with you buddy?**
**Alright, nine lives! - But at the rate you're using them up...?**

*He pauses. There is the SOUND of a car coming, in the other direction. He immediately assumes the hitchhiker's stance, the cat under one arm. Car passes him by without stopping, never slackening speed. He looks after it, looks once back, then starts trudging slowly south himself on foot. ..*

DISSOLVE:

---

269.    *DESERT HIGHWAY- ON Ro and the cat, walking. He turns, car motor SOUNDS. He waits. A car drives up and stops, its motor running; it is the mustang, of course, Helen inside. She gives him an ironic, interrogatory glance.*

**RO**
(*clumsy imitation of the old lady*)
**"Took you longer than I figured."**
(*he gets in the car*)

**Constitutional. My friend and I never miss.**
*(The cat is still. Helen not moving. The moment charged)*
**Hey lady?  Do you happen to know a poet named
Hopkins?  Gerald Manley Hopkins?"**

**This retrieved phrase,- scooped up outrageously from the past-
breaks Helen's mood.  She smiles, puts the car in gear, starts off.
But there is a certain tension between the sally; a certain irony in
her response.**

## DISSOLVE:

---

270.    *INT. MUSTANG- MID-MORNING.  Very very hot.  ON Ro and
Helen. Ro is now driving, the cat dozing on the windshield ,
Helen reading from a little booklet.*

### HELEN (v.o.)
**"From mid-morning to two or three P.M...."**

271.    AT THE SKY. The sun is burning, the blue is almost too intense
to contemplate.

### HELEN (v.o.)
**"...the traveler, new to the desert, would do well to..."**

272.    INT. SMALL TOWN ARIZONA MOVIE HOUSE. ON Ro and
Helen, seated side by side, escaping the desert heat in the air-
cooled interior, the cat on Helen's lap. O.S. SOUND of Sousa
marches.

### HELEN (v.o.)
**"...grab whatever shelter is at hand..."**

273.    MOVIE SCREEN. Advertising placard: "**Levine's Clothing
Mart. Clearance Sale:  Up To One-Third Off. <u>Third and Main.
Open Evenings.</u>**" Another placard: "**U.S. Marine Corps Invites
You To Consider <u>Advantages Of A Military Career. Travel!
Education! Service! Contact Sgt. William Traynor, Braintree
Bank Building.  1:15PM. Thursday .</u>**"

274.    Ro and Helen. She is no longer looking at the screen, but
gazing at Ro. She traces the line of his face with her fingers.

The sensual excitement rising.  O.S. Sousa march BLARING
LOUD.

275.     MOVIE SCREEN- another advertisement.  "Kellington
         Abdominal Supports. Our Regional Expert, Mr.
         Emanuel Vortzman .Will Be In Braintree Next Monday . Please
         Phone YMCA For Appointment.  We Carry A Complete Line Of
         Trusses . Service Guaranteed."

276.     ON Ro and Helen in their seats. The intensity of her gaze at
         him, forces him to look at her- their glances lock. The march
         PLAYS on O.S.

277.     MOVIE SCREEN- placard: "Braintree Chapter Of Alcoholics
         Anonymous Announces Its Semi-Monthly Meeting . 8 PM.
         Braintree Methodist Church.  All Invited."

278.     Ro and Helen. As Helen suddenly gets up deliberately, and
         makes for the exit.  Ro follows her.

279.     EXT. SMALL TOWN MOVIE HOUSE. ON Finnegan, tethered to
         the cashier's window, licking from a bowl of milk.  Helen and Ro
         appear, Helen in F.G. She passes straight INTO CAMERA and
         O.S. Ro stops, kneels, retrieves the cat. He starts forward.

280.     ON SMALL TOWN HOTEL - across the street. The green
         mustang parked conspicuously in front. As Helen, not looking
         back once, strides directly forward, and into the hotel.

281.     ON Ro. Slowing crossing the street, and standing there, the pet
         in his arms, looking up.

282.     SECOND FLOOR HOTEL WINDOW. After a second, the
         shade pulls up, the window is flung open, Helen appears for a
         second looking down. Then withdraws.

283.     SIDEWALK - ON Ro. He doesn't move. He turns and looks
         down the street.

284.     LONG ANGLE - RO'S POV- A BUS STATION.
         Busses are parked. One is loading.

285.     ON Ro, very CLOSE now. He still hasn't moved.
         Indecision patent in his eyes.

286. ON HELEN- SHOT NUMBER "M" IN PROLOGUE- AS SHE WAS AT THE BEGINNING OF THE FILM. THERE FOLLOWS THE EXACT SEQUENCE , STARTING WITH "M" IN THE PROLOGUE, THE SAME SEQUENCE IMAGES, LEADING TO THE TERRIBLE CRASH: THE CRACKED CLOCK , THE FREEZING SILENCE .

287. MEDIUM FULL - BACK OF THE TIPPED TRUCK. It is loaded - and this is the first time we've seen it- with huge 100 gallon drums; it is pitched on one side, some drums seem to be loose from their moorings. A SOUND- a LOUD eat's cry- wells up from the drums...

288. MEDIUM CLOSE- ON Finnegan. Crouched warily among the drums, on the floor of the truck, where he seems to have been tossed. A small liquid puddle is around him, he is soaked in it. It seems to bother him; he gets out of there, climbs up on the drum, perched ...

289. SWOLLEN STREAM- perhaps a tributary of the Gila River, glittering in the moonlight. As we watch, a water-soaked log floats by: a small body hurdles on to it; it is the cat, liberating itself from the back of the truck, now tensely balanced on the floating debris going downstream. There is a sudden, shocking, terrifying second CRASH ...

290. ON THE STREAM: the green mustang has tumbled, from balancing on the bridge, into the water; it is upside down, its cab squashed, no movement whatsoever. The cat sails by in F.G....

The forlornness, the lack of any human movement, of any visible sign of life, is excruciating.

291. A BEND IN THE BANK: barren. Suddenly the cat leaps on to it. CLOSE on the animal: it seems uncomfortable. A LOUD WHINE, a feline cry. It turns. It begins vigorously, in the manner of cats, to lick itself thoroughly down, scrubbing and licking that aggravating coat. (Aggravated by what?) ZOOM IN very close to the cat's image, licking itself. FREEZE FRAME.

# TAURUS

"ACCENTUATE THE POSITIVE SIDE,

AVOID FLIGHTS OF FANCY...

WHATEVER YOU DO,

BE DOWN TO EARTH..."

292.   *EXT. YUMA, ARIZONA AIRPORT- DAY. A plane has landed,*
*and passengers are descending ,among them Nicholas: he*
*looks radically altered - he is wearing a plain suit, no clerical*
*collar, obviously hasn't shaved, gaunt. CAMERA PANS him*
*over to a YOUNG BUSINESS TYPE, young-middle-aged,*
*glasses, briefcase in hand. He is a representative of a car*
*rental company.*

**CAR REPRESENTATIVE**
**Doctor McAllister?**
*(he goes up, shakes Nicholas' hand)*
**Roy Treadwell. The man who spoke to you on the phone.**
*(as they both move off together, Nicholas walking woodenly)*

**Terribly sorry. I mean, that we have to meet**
**under such unhappy circumstances ...**

DISSOLVE:

___

293.   INT. MOVING CAR- on Arizona road. Nicholas is sitting in the
front seat next to Mr. Treadwell, who is driving.

**CAR REPRESENTATIVE**
**No question ,the truck's fault. You can tell by**
**the skid marks, out of control...**

294.   MOVING- FROM THE WINDOW OF THE CAR. Showing a
roadblock ahead, cars being routed onto another side road.

**CAR REPRESENTATIVE (v.o.)**
**There is a small technical question. I hate to bring this.**
**Apparently, your wife ...**

We are now approaching an obviously monitored area.
SOUND of a huge crane operating O.S.

**CAR REPRESENTATIVE (v.o.)**
**...intended to leave the vehicle off at the state line...**

295.   INT. CAR- ON Nicholas, alone, staring in horror out the
window.

**CAR REPRESENTATIVE (v.o.)**
**But I don't think, in this instance,**
**we need be too sticky about that.**

295.    REVERSE ANGLE . WHAT NICHOLAS SEES: The overturned truck, in process of slowly being hoisted up on a huge tow truck. Its top has been sealed. Policemen are standing along the road.

296.    GREEN MUSTANG: evidently hauled onto a bank, its wheels askew, looking like the ghastly wreck it is, its cabin stove in from the force of the fall.

297.    RATHER FULL- THE CREEK. A row of Indians, Piutes- stand there stolid- with a row of cattle behind them. In front, at spaced intervals- are highway policemen "guarding" the creek , preventing anyone from coming too close.

298.    *THREE OR FOUR ALERT YOUNG MEN- obviously technical experts. They are performing a sort of strange ritual. They are walking around the area, carrying walkie-talkies, and swinging their portable Geiger counters. At this point, of course, we don't know who they are or what they are actually doing. The Geiger counter CLICK for normal background radiation is a sporadic cluster, a desultory rattle, something like the typewriter keys being slowly punched in uneven rhythm. This SOUND- we now here distinctly.*

**CAR REPRESENTATIVE (v.o.)**
**On behalf of the company,**

299.    *TWO SHOT- ON Nicholas and car representative, now on foot, walking slowly through the heavily guarded area.*

**CAR REPRESENTATIVE**
**I'd like to offer our extreme condolences and sympathy ...**

*Nicholas doesn't seem to respond. He walks dully, straight ahead. A policeman points out a sight, giving them directions . Nicholas turns, shakes hands with Mr. Treadwell, leaving him there, and walks on ahead , CAMERA staying on Nicholas, losing the car representative.*

300.    INT. LARGE MILITARY TENT- an improvised "command" post set up nearby. As Nicholas is passed through by a guard, and stops short. Looking up, staring , bewildered, obviously in a state of shock.

301. *LONG IMPROVISED TABLE at opposite end of the tent. A kind of improvised stage. Behind this table sit FOUR MEN; they are holding an "informal" press conference. Each has a hand-lettered name card in front of him. They are the following*

*DR. BILLINGS, a representative of the AEC; MR. MANSON, a representative of the power company ; DR. MARTINEZ, a weathered ,white -haired old public health doctor, cradling his inseparable pet Siamese cat, and smoking a pipe; and SHERIFF ANGELO PETRI, the local law enforcement officer for the area , in uniform, an Indian, a crony and longtime friend of Dr. Martinez. The questions come at these men from O.S., but it is all very informal, full of a certain feverish hustle, and improvisation.*

**DR. BILLINGS**

**...I'd be the first to admit we were lucky. One drum slightly damaged, seepage apparently minimal, confined to the bottom of the truck ... Of course, Contingency Monitoring Procedures are being carried out. But there's no indication of any immediate concern ...**

There is an O.S. question, in Piute tongue. Dr. Billings looks to Dr. Martinez to translate.

**DR. MARTINEZ**
(*to Billings*)
**He wants to know how long before his people can use the creek - they've got a hundred head of cattle baking out there, you know...**

302. LITTLE WOODEN TABLE near corner of tent. On it, stark, and riveting, several articles of clothing belonging to Helen- cloth jacket, gloves, pull-on sweater. After a second Nicholas comes INTO SHOT; he is staring down at these things. He can't move.

**DR. BILLINGS (v.o.)**

**Soon as we complete our monitoring procedures -though as I said, there doesn't seem to be anything to worry about...**

303. ON THE PANEL, featuring the sheriff, who turns in annoyance to the AEC man.

**SHERIFF PETRI**
**Why all this hullabaloo then?**
**Tying up traffic?  Bottlenecking the area?...**

### MR. MANSON
(*calmly*}
We're just programmed, you might say, to err on the side of caution. But you have my reassurances -

### DR. MARTINEZ
(*an explosion*)
Reassurances!
(profanely *eloquent*)

Hell, we've been plastered with "reassurances" for years!. ..We were reassured left and right that the tailings -you know, the waste - from those closed-down uranium mines were safe. And now we're having to evacuate the area. Ten years later! (looking directly at the company representative, Mr. Manson) I'd like to know what that truck was doing out here alone, unconvoyed ,going hell bent for leather, on an unprogrammed routing ...?

### MR. MANSON
Believe me, we want to know just as much as you, Dr. Martinez. We've already got an investigation going ...As a physician, however, you ought to be able to appreciate the Human Factor; I mean, anyone can have a heart attack at any time...

### DR. MARTINEZ
(*an eloquent peroration*)
I'm not speakin' as a "physician," I'm speakin' as a plain citizen!
(a sort of eloquent summation)
Face it, "environment" has become the political code word for apple pie, open bowels, and God knows what other virtues.! Everyone's for it, we're drowning in the goddam consensus. But meanwhile, far as I can see - business's going on mostly as usual.
(directly to Mr. Manson)
(*continued*)

304. Cont.

### DR. MARTINEZ
(*continued*)
You keep buildin' those plants of yours, by the year two thousand - if we're still here -we're going to have three thousand nuclear hearses lugging millions of curies around, to be stuffed in the landscape! Man'd be a damn fool not to be scared!

*Another O.S. question in Piute tongue.*

## SHERIFF
*(to Dr. Billings, translating with a certain relish}*
**He wants to know how many of his people are going to die, and can they be buried in the usual place?**

## DR. BILLINGS
*(looking directly at Martinez, with a certain anger)*
**See? Example of what I mean, gentlemen! Absolutely unjustified panic reaction! Now I've been absolutely candid about the facts, but you know as well as I, in a situation of this kind, we've got to cool things, keep people's imaginations from running away with them...**
*(to the Sheriff, looking at Martinez however)*
**You tell him, Sheriff- no, "reassure" him- as I've already explained, nobody's in any danger whatsoever. Only one container was ruptured, all the liquid was contained in the truck. To have gotten contaminated you'd have had to climb up in the dark, and dunked yourself ...**

## DR. MARTINEZ
**What if it was ingested? <u>Swallowed</u> , - in plain English?**

*This question- so preposterous, on the face of it-provokes a laugh from Mr. Manson.*

304.  Cont.
## MR. MANSON
**Really, Dr. Martinez...**

## DR. BILLINGS
*(mock serious)*
**No, it's all right.  We're here to answer questions, - he asked us a question.**
*(ironic recital, to Martinez)*
**If somebody clambered up. And then managed -God knows how - to  scoop up some of  that  effluent. And he actually "swallowed" some- he'd have to have a taste for boiling sulphuric acid, of course- why then, you could have a lethal situation because the stuff, as you know, is an iodine analogue , it builds up in the Thyroid. You'd be a sort of walking X-ray machine, long as you lased.  Jumping out of a window ,of course, would be a much less arduous way of accomplishing  the same thing...**

305.   ON Nicholas, seated in a chair, numbly, near the small wooden
       table. He holds in his lap Helen's debris. His expression,
       still paralyzed.

### SHERIFF (v.o.)
**When can we start draggin' for the woman , Dr. Billings?**

### DR. BILLINGS (v.o.)
**Soon as I get my clearances, Sheriff.**
**Believe me, we're working on it fast as we can.**

306.   EXT. STREAM-the line of monitors, FOUR MEN, are slowly
       walking in it, near the bank; two have walkie- talkies.

307.   THE LINE OF INDIANS, stolid, standing in front of the cattle,
       waiting. The cops in front of them.

308.   Nicholas, Dr. Martinez, with his Siamese cat in his arms, and the
       Sheriff- a small group watching .

309.   Dr. Billings, holding a walkie-talkie, standing by the bank, intent.

310.   MEDIUM VIEW OF STREAM, showing two monitors, one with
       walkie-talkie, both with Geiger counters- in shallow water. We
       HEAR the desultory and unmistakable CLICKING of the
       counters. CAMERA CLOSES on the monitor with the
       walkie-talkie.

### MONITOR
(*into walkie-talkie*)
**How about it, Roger?**

### WALKIE-TALK! E
(*answering*)
**What have you got?**

### MONITOR
**Eighty-six point four MR's.  Variation of four point seven-eight.**
**Two thousand eleven meters from IP. N by NE.**

### WALKIE- TALKIE
**What do you figure?**

## MONITOR
Well, we've already doubled the minimals. Besides, the Indians are
waitin' for their creek, the cops are waitin' to drag bottom, and I feel
like I'm catching pneumonia....I'd say we
ought to admit we were plain damn fool lucky. Go home,
give the TP department a kick in the ass!

## WALKIE- TALKIE
Okay.  C'mon in out of the hot sun!

*The monitor turns, and moves back downstream, and OUT OF
CAMERA . We are now watching the turbulent waters; CAMERA
MOVES FORWARD deliberately -evenly- and finally comes to rest on
the little bluff where the cat, Finnegan, had jumped , shockingly
recognizable in the afternoon sun. HOLD.*

## DISSOLVE:

---

*311.     INT. HEADQUARTERS  TENT- LATE AFTERNOON.   It is
pouring rain and THUNDER- one of those terrific flash flood storms
which designate the southwest. Inside the tent, Dr. Martinez and Sheriff
Petri are seated over a game of chess, passing the time. Several
uniformed Indians- part of the Sheriffs squad- are standing around.
Nicholas sits in a wood chair, next to the little wooden table, vacant.  His
wife's effects in his lap.*

## SHERIFF
*(to Nicholas)*
Don't worry, we'll find her, doctor...
sometimes it just takes a little time...

## DR. MARTINEZ
Move, you slow witted redskin!
*(to Nicholas- attempt at diversion)*
What do you think of a supposedly mature individual, who swears
by everything holy he was chased down the road by two flying
saucers in broad daylight, eight months ago, in this very location?

## SHERIFF
That means he's losing!
*(to Nicholas)*
He always brings up the F.O. incident whenever he's losing...

130

DR. MARTINEZ
True or false?  You saw it or not?
SHERIFF
(*wearily*)
I saw it.  My wife saw it. Two busloads of kids, four airline pilots,
and the undertaker of Mitchell County saw it!  What can you do?
We're all crazy, call out the loony bin...!
(*grim*)
Move!


312.     ANOTHER ANGLE- on entrance to tent.  As three hippie
         pilgrims come in, soaking wet.  ONE GIRL and TWO BOYS. All
         have long hair, and all are dressed, naturally, like Indians. There
         is an instant terrific hostility in the room toward these only-too-
         frequent vagabonds on southwestern roads.

312.  Cont.
BOY
Man!...At least we know what Noah was rapping about, right?

GIRL
Hey look...Indians!

*She goes up, speaks some Piute words to the two uniformed Indians.*
*They disdain to answer; blatant with hostility. The Sheriff gets up.*

SHERIFF
Okay.  O.U.T.!  Out!

BOY
It's the flood, Sheriff!  You want to drown us in the flood?

GIRL
(*urging him toward the door*)
Let's go, Ronnie...why argue with these dime store types? ...

BOY
Wait!...

*He holds up his hand, very dramatic; he walks straight over to where*
*Nicholas is sitting. Nobody knows what's up.*

313.     ANGLE ON NICHOLAS, as the action focuses toward him.


131

### BOY
(*his eyes close for a second, his voice excited*)
**The letter H. I get it, man, strong!...
Brown hair, medium height, and the letter H...**

### SHERIFF
**If you guys are really shopping for a vagrancy rap...**

313. Cont.

### GIRL
(*to Nicholas, ignoring Sheriff*)
**He's a spook, Mister. I know it's crazy.
But he really, like, "gets" things...**

### BOY
**This man is looking for somebody -
Brown hair, female, the letter "H". Right?**
(*concentrating, shaking his head*)
**If you're looking around here -forget it!  She's someplace
else. And danger ...I get danger loud and clear. ..**

### SHERIFF
(*sighing*)
**O-Kay...**

(*to one of the other deputies*)
**Take 'em in, Clarence...The usual, Vagrancy.  Code 1-0-3.**

### NICHOLAS
**No!**
(rousing himself)

*He suddenly takes out a bill from his pocket, and hands it to the boy; the boy looks at it, shakes his head.*

### BOY
**Uh uh.**
(*putting the bill back on the table*)
**Never take money for using the spirit, man!...
you do that, it'll go right away - right?**
(*to the Sheriff and other Indians*)

*He makes an Indian farewell sign.  The trio of kids vanishes.*

**<u>SHERIFF</u>**
(sighing, looking at Martinez)
**Don't look at me, all I did was see a Flying Saucer!**


313. Cont.

He leaves the tent; the rain has noticeably slackened. Nicholas, after hesitant moment, goes after him. CAMERA CLOSES IN on the figure of the grizzled old doctor, pipe in mouth, Siamese in his arms, staring. CLOSE to the figure of the pet cat, and HOLD, FREEZING FRAME. We suddenly HEAR, O.S., the familiar feint clicking of the Geiger counter.

# LIBRA

"BEWARE! IF YOU ARE NOT CAREFUL TODAY,
YOUR IMAGINATION COULD LEAD
YOU FAR AFIELD..."

313.     INT. PIUTE HOGAN, somewhere in the middle of the desolate Piute reservation country. SLOW PAN. On the primitive interior of this Hogan, no one IN CAMERA. It is morning.

### HELEN (v.o.)
**...just a run-of-the-mill nightmare, of course...**

We now come to Finnegan, the cat, nestled next to Helen, herself: she is curled up, exhausted, sleeping, eyes shut, very restive in sleep. She looks as if she had been through hell - bruised - scratched -clothes somewhat torn.  Smudged.

### HELEN (v.o.)
**...full of the usual imaginary catastrophes-accident, wilderness, savages, etcetera. But I knew I'd be glad to wake up...**
*(she opens her eyes suddenly; stares).*

REVERSE ANGLE- squatted semi-circle of INDIAN WOMEN, somberly regarding her. Their looks are very grave, weighty with dignity. They are, of course, an uncanny sight.

### HELEN (v.o.)
**...to the blessed boredom of my everyday life!...**

### DISSOLVE:

---

314.     *EXT. HOGAN -A SMALL CLEARING. Helen is seated on a stump, sipping hot soup, reading a note. This is a rather CLOSE ANGLE, so we can see her expression as she reads.*

315.  Cont.

### RO (v.o.)
**"Dear Mamma, alias Aunt Polly, etc. - Don't flip, but I decided it might be less complicated all around if I just lit out, as Huck Finn used to say , for the Territory... Please take good care of Finney- he's only on loan, remember- and for   God sakes, let's both of us take an oath: No more internal combustion engines, period.  Love.  R..."**

316.     GROUP OF PIUTE WOMEN, the same ones we saw before, squatted in a semi-circle, still gravely considering this visitor.

RO (v.o.)
"P.S. These people, they're Piutes- pronounced Pi-yuu-tees
- will return you to the 20th century, - if you really insist.
(Don't worry- it's always closer than we think!")

317.     ON Helen. As she looks up from the paper and smiles.
         The cat in her lap.

DISSOLVE:

---

318.     EXT. DESOLATE BEAUTIFUL DESERT COUNTRY, showing
         Helen on horseback. She's worn. She's holding Finney. She
         has a very detached air.

HELEN (v.o.)
Obviously I was alive by some sort of miracle...

319.     SEVERAL OTHER HORSES WITH INDIAN WOMEN on them.
         Moving. They are guiding Helen along the barren path...

HELEN (v.o.)
...which I owed perhaps, largely to him...

320.     CLOSE- on Finnegan- being jostled along in the saddle
         in front of Helen.

HELEN (v.o.)
...I also knew there must be a terrible scene –
I'll have to face up to, sooner or later...

321.     VERY CLOSE- ON Helen, gazing around her at the beautiful
         landscape: the colors; the wilderness. A sort of smile.

321.  Cont.
HELEN (v.o.)
...at the same time I felt absurdly peaceful. As if a part of me
was still asleep. Not only what had been a nightmare...

322.     A SWEEP OF THE TERRITORY , FROM HELEN'S POV. It is
         just as beautiful as described.

**HELEN (v.o.)**
**...had turned into one of those garden variety visions of**
**Shangri-la. Where everything...**

323.    ANOTHER VIEW OF LANDSCAPE- FROM INDIAN WOMEN'S
POV. Their faces in F.G.

**HELEN (v.o.)**
**...faces, auras, landscapes- seemed so much richer,**
**more vivid, than anything ...**

324.    RATHER FULL ON HELEN- MOVING - jogging along, in a kind
of trance.

**HELEN (v.o.)**
**...you knew you'd be able to experience after you woke up!...**

DISSOLVE:

---

325.    *INT. REMOTE CROSSROADS TRADING POST -little more*
*than a shack. Showing Helen at a phone, the cat in her arms,*
*trying to ring a response from the operator with a little handle,*
*and failing.*

**HELEN (v.o.)**
**No doubt, that explains why- though the doctors, in their**
**mundane way, later to call it "shock reaction' -**

*She gives up on the phone, and comes out, CAMERA PANNING her*
*through the trading post, and HOLDING on her.*

**HELEN (v.o.)**
**I apparently went on...**

326.    *EXT. TINY TRADING POST. An old touring car is there, a mail*
*car. A WOMAN seated within, and the door open, as Helen*
*goes out and gets into it and Indian helping her with her things.*

**HELEN (v.o.)**
**...trying to keep on "dreaming," for as long as I could...**

*Helen gets in the car. It drives off.*

138

DISSOLVE:

---

327.    INT. MAIL CAR- ON Helen and the knarled, middle-aged,
weather-beaten mail lady dressed in man's clothing. A very
sour woman; expression as if she were eating a lemon.

### MAIL LADY
**Do you mind moving that animal? I'm allergic to cats...**

*Helen picks up the cat which has been between them, and puts it over
on her side of the seat. The cat gives a listless cry.*

### MAIL LADY
**They cause cancer too, you know. I read about it somewhere ...**

328.    MEDIUM CLOSE on Finnegan: lying there on the seat. He
definitely looks peaked; not much movement. Patches of hair
on gone here and there.

### MAIL LADY (v.o.)
**There's this scientist in England, he found some
sort of definite link-up, cats and viruses...**

329.    RATHER CLOSE on the seat between the two women :
showing the hair that has already fallen out of the animal ...

### MAIL LADY (v.o.)
**Not that I want to alarm you or anything ...
(another tone: furious) Goddamit!
Look! Hair all over the front seat!...**

DISSOLVE:

---

330.    EXT. SMALL TOWN, LARGER CROSSROADS, WITH A BUS
STATION STOP. Helen sits there on a bench, the cat crouched
by her feet. She still has a strangely detached air. After a
second, an OLD MAN- obviously a character- suspendered,
toothless, but very keen-eyed, ambles INTO SHOT. He looks
down at Finnegan. He looks around furtively, then back at
Helen. His name is AMBROSE.

**AMBROSE**
Wanna sell that animal-lady?


**WOMAN (v.o.)**
(*calling*)
Ambrose!


**AMBROSE**
(*hastily*)
I'll give you fifteen bucks cash!
(*he kneels down, stretches out a hand; withdraws it with a
small yelp, as the cat lashes out with a paw*)
All right, twenty then!  But hurry up before-


He looks O.S., then runs off and OUT OF VIEW himself. In a second a
WOMAN appears, staring down, looking at Helen, a little out of breath,
apologetic. She is middle-aged, motherly, sombreroed, and matriarchal.


**WOMAN**
Apologize, madam.  My brother-in-law ...
Ever since his wife died, he
(*she whirls a finger at her ear, indicating lunacy*)
...keeps thinking she's going to come meow-ing back in the form of
a cat.  Honest to God, I'm so sick and tired of the sight of cats...


**AMBROSE (v.o.)**
Tried to bite me- that <u>proves</u> it, don't it?
Offer her fifty dollars, cash on the barrelhead!


330.  Cont.

**WOMAN**
(*sadly*)
Damn fool doesn't even own the underwear
he's walking around  in...
(*she walks O.S.*)
**AMBROSE (v.o.)**
All right, sixty-five then.  Last and final offer!...


331.    ON Finnegan- CLOSE- at Helen's feet. A bowl of milk is placed
next to him. He looks at it, he doesn't move.


DISSOLVE:

---

332.  INT. PHONE BOOTH INSIDE BUS STATION.  ON Helen and
      cat, squeezed together. She is still talking on a long distance
      line, having to shout.


### HELEN
**I'll speak to whoever's on the line then.
But please, don't cut me off again operator...**
*(pause)*
**...Hello? Could I please speak to the Reverend Nicholas--
Are you sure?...But didn't he leave any message, or say--
oh...I see...**

*A MAN in a bus driver's uniform has come INTO SHOT, is pounding on
the door of the booth, gesturing with his hand: hurry up, we've got to go.
She hangs up the phone.*


### DISSOLVE:

---

333.  INT. TOURING CROSS-COUNTRY  BUS- full of sightseers.  ON
      Helen.  MEDIUM SHOT from the waist up: she seems to be busy
      with some unpleasant thing going on O.S....

### AD LIB PROTESTS OF PASSENGERS

**"Look, lady- please. I mean, we appreciate
your problem, but this is a public conveyance ..."**

**"How do you expect her to get a cat to
throw up in a brown paper bag?..."**

**"Mommie, mommie, can I pet the pussycat?..."**

333.  Cont.
**"Stay away, Caroline. If it don't act rabid, that don't mean it
ain't. With cats, you never can tell...**

**"Ride-sick, that's all. Everybody knows
cats get ride-sick once in a while..."**

"Worms. I've seen it plenty of times.
Cats pick up worms quicker than a dog can pee..."

DISSOLVE:

_____

334.   INT. BUS- ON Helen, dozing.  So is the cat, seemingly, in her lap.  CLOSE ON her face.

335.   A SCRIM: what she sees- Nicholas, rather blurred, before the pulpit, earnestly intoning.

**NICHOLAS (v.o.)**
**...what immortal hand or eye could frame thy fearful symmetry ...**

DISSOLVE:

_____

336.   EXT. COUNTER- BUS REST STOP - ALONG A TRAVELLED ROAD: we are heading up the Arizona desert country. CLOSE ON Finnegan, looking up at something O.S. The slits of his pupils very large in view.

**NICHOLAS (v.o.)**
**"In what distant deeps or skies, Burnt the fire of thine eyes..."**

337.   VERY CLOSE- MODEL OF PHANTOM JET, MOUNTED ON WALL.

**NICHOLAS (v.o.)**
**"On what wings dare he aspire..."**

_Finnegan suddenly appears, having jumped up on top of plane, crouched there!_

338.   _WAITRESS BEHIND COUNTER- MEDIUM SHOT. She looks exasperated . She moves over to remove the cat from the display._

338.  Cont.

**NICHOLAS (v.o.)**
**"...what the hand dare seize the fire..."**

*The waitress pulls back, as the cat lashes out with a paw.*

339.    EXT. PARKED BUS- QUEUE OF PASSENGERS *waiting to re-enter. ON OLDER MAN with sketch pad. He is sketching away.*

### NICHOLAS (v.o.)
**"...and what shoulder and what art..."**

340.    CLOSE- the sketch pad:  it is a rough sketch of Finnegan, crouched, eyes glazed.

### NICHOLAS (v.o.)
**"...could twist the sinews of thy heart..."**

341.    INT. BUS  ON Helen and Finnegan.  The cat featured in F.G., Helen looking out the window.

### NICHOLAS (v.o.)
**"...what the hammer, what the chain...
In what furnace was thy brain... What the anvil. .."**

342.    INT. RURAL VETERINARIAN'S WAITING ROOM. VERY CLOSE on Finnegan. Being carried in arms, sheathed in a veterinarian's coat, along a counter, protesting slightly ...

### NICHOLAS (v.o.)
**"...what dread grasp...
dare it's deadly terrors clasp..."**

*CAMERA PULL BACK.  Helen is revealed, worn, confronting the veterinarian, who seems very exasperated. He places Finnegan on the counter, takes out a hypo from a prepared counter.*

### VETERINARIAN
(*sternly*)

**I don't want to lecture you, ma'am.  But frankly I'm fed up with folks who dote on their pets, tote 'em around spoilin' 'em half to death, and then come to me to repair the damage!...**
(*he grasps the hypo*)
**Let's keep a firm hold now.**

342.   Cont.

*He gives the animal a shot in the rump; naturally the cat howls.
He takes away the hypo.*

143

## VETERINARIAN

That'll take care of the distemper- should have been tended to long ago. But he's definitely been poisoned - some damn fool thing somebody fed him, I suspect... I'll take him back, give him a cathartic, and if you do like I say, he'll probably be
okay in a day or two.
(*a stern summation*)
Providing, of course, you start treatin' him sensible . Cats are hearty enough, as animals go, but in the end, they ain't no more mortal than you or me!

*Veterinarian exits, toting the cat with him. Helen sits wearily down on the bench. She is tired, obviously - yet still retains that air of uncanny detachment, a sort of surreal calm. CAMERA SLOWLY RISES above Helen, losing her, and comes to rest on one of a series of idealized sentimental framed portraits of circus animals: we are looking at three tigers in a cage; they stare at us with malevolent eyes. Coincident with this image: the terrible inexorable increasing RATTLE of the rising Curie count- it HOLDS for a few seconds. FREEZE FRAME.*

# VIRGO

"REMEMBER SEEING IS
NOT ALWAYS BELIEVING."

343.     INT. HEALING ROOM OF SMALL SPANISH-AMERICAN CHURCH- SMALL NEW MEXICAN TOWN. Penasco, was the model in mind. MEDIUM SHOT on Ro: he is standing there , writing in a little notebook, his eyes faced toward a wall, a quizzical expression. His data-gathering stare. REVERSE ANGLE on the wall, massive white-washed stone. There are crutches tacked up, canes, leg braces, spinal supports . All the discarded paraphernalia of cured cripples . CAMERA MOVES CLOSER ; we can see some of the legends attached : Over a crutch - "I was a cripple for 12 years until the Lord cured me on June 13. 1962. All praise to Jesus Christ. William Sacks, Tulsa. Oklahoma."

Under a leg brace- "In this room. on July 2. 1958, I underwent the Lord's divine healing through the intervention of His servant, the blessed Guadalupe . Marian McKenzie , Irvington. Illinois."

Under spinal supports- "Gracias 'ADios ,jo peudo cominar sin apoyo la prima vez en quinze anos!"


344.     RATHER FULL ON HEALING ROOM. As KELLY comes in, a young girl about 19 years old- pale, taught, tense , with a fierce ready-to-lash-out look in her eyes. Very thin, high cheek bones, tan coloring ; a flawless light coffee skin. She would have been extraordinarily beautiful, except she is dehydrated by anxiety, fatigue, and plain malnutrition . Long beautiful hair in braids, long patchwork skirt, dirty; long, thin beautiful hands. She could be from anywhere. A commune, a Pueblo village ,even a big city hippie hutch. The lines on her face show how close to hysteria she is. But she has herself- by some superhuman effort - under a modicum of control.

She is, obviously, under the concentration of a thought-out purpose. She is also about 6 or 7 months pregnant; and the pathos of this fact is patently enormous; her stomach bulges in front of her; under her long skirt, her thin legs seem like spindles.


**KELLY**
*(to Ro)*
**Hey...**
*(he looks at her)*
How about, instructions?
**I mean, don't they give you, like, any instructions or anything?**

**RO**
**I don't know...**
*(shruggin, friendly)*
**You're supposed to be on your own, I guess ...**


344. Cont.
*Kelly looks around. She suddenly moves forward; takes one of the little crosses under the great central heating shrine, and shoves it furtively underneath her blouse.*

345.     ON KELLY- her eyes looking at Ro. They say- okay, you saw me. What do you propose doing about it?

346.     ON RO -looking at her. Speechless.

347.     *EXT.THE LITTLE CHURCH. A beaten up motorcycle is parked there, loaded down with a vagabond bundle, tied to the rear luggage rack. Kelly comes running INTO SHOT, gets on the motorcycle, leaps on the starter peddle ...*

348.     *EXT. CHURCH ENTRANCE, as Ro comes out, crystallized by the whole thing: the sight of her, her condition, her theft, her imminent getaway. As he looks, intent, the ROAR O.S. of the motorcycle starts.*

349.     RO'S POV. The motorcycle roaring off around the bend of the dusty road.

DISSOLVE:

---

350.     *EXT. DUSTY NEW MEXICAN ROAD- AFTERNOON. ON Ro. He has been tramping quite awhile without a ride- obviously tired , hungry, and aggravated . He stops suddenly, staring.*

351.     THE MOTORCYCLE- PARKED IN A LITTLE CLUMP OF BUSHES BY THE SIDE OF THE ROAD.

**KELLY (v.o.)**

**C'mon! It's not as if I'm asking such a big deal, right? I mean, if You could do all those other groovy things-**

**For <u>You</u>, this ought to be nothing!**

147

352.   *ON Ro- MOVING. He hurries down the road, past the motorcycle, into the bushes. Then stops dead. Staring.*

353.   *RO'S POV. On a bluff, about 15 or 20 feet high - Kelly. She is standing there, talking to the little cross, as if it were something alive.*

353.   Cont.

### KELLY
**All I want, - just jog the damn thing loose, that's all.**
(*logical*)
**I mean - it's a sin to have it and not want it - right? And we both know I'm a cop-out when it comes to heights.**
(*she closes her eyes tightly , advancing to the edge of the bluff, clutching the cross*)
**So if you'll just give me a little push...**

### RO (v.o.)
**Hey!...**

*Kelly jumps!*

### DISSOLVE:

---

354.   BOTTOM OF THE BLUFF. On Ro and Kelly. Ro is working, bandaging a sprained ankle. Kelly's face is set in a 1-won't-talk grimace; she allows him to bind her ankle, but gives no other sign -neither gratitude nor approbation .

### RO
**Try to stand. Let's see what happens...**

*She gets up.  She tries to walk . She can hardly hobble. Obviously a bad sprain.*

### RO
**Obviously you need something better.**
**I mean any professional could...**

148

KELLY
No!

*She looks at him. Her eyes burn.*

DISSOLVE:

---

355.     DUSK. MOVING SHOT on Ro and Kelly, driving down the
         road. Ro is at the wheel , Kelly seated behind, her pregnant
         stomach pressing against him. She is silent, sullen.

355.  Cont.
RO (v.o.)
**Memo:**
**From: R. Williams!**
**To: R. Williams!**
**Dear Saint Sebastian ...**

356.     *INT. ROADSIDE COUNTRY STORE, as Ro collects a bag of
         groceries as he pays at the counter. He turns and begins
         walking towards the door, CAMERA MOVING with him.*

RO (v.o.)
**Wise up, Samaritan. You just got off one hook- right?**

357.     *EXT. STORE, as Ro emerges, CAMERA MOVING him over to
         the motorcycle, on which Kelly sits, sullen, waiting. He hands
         her the groceries, gets on the bike.*

RO (v.o.)
**What the hell do you think you're doing,**
**playing Albert Schweitzer to a...**

*The bike starts off, MOVING SHOT on Kelly, clinging on behind.*

RO (v.o.)
**...teenage female runaway...**

358.     EXT. MESA- NIGHT- SOMEWHERE IN NEW MEXICO.   ON
Kelly, wolfing down food, cheese and crackers, perhaps.

### RO (v.o.)
**...half-starved...**

Ro comes INTO SHOT; Kelly backs off, a knife in her hand - a cheese knife, perhaps - ready to "defend" herself.

### RO (v.o.)
**...wild ...**

*He brushes the knife aside. Bends down to examine her foot.*

### RO (v.o.)
**...crippled ...**

359.    Featuring Kelly, her maternal bulge in F.G.,
        glaring down at his ministrations.


359.  Cont.

### RO (v.o.)
**...six months pregnant...**

### DISSOLVE:

---

360.    EXT. ANOTHER PART OF THE MESA- On Kelly, she is mixing some stuff in a glass, pouring powders, pills perhaps, hastily, even furtively.

### RO (v.o.)
**...and hell-bent to abort the baby...**
She looks off, and starts to drink the terrible stuff with a grimace.
...or kill herself...

*Ro comes INTO SHOT, wrestling to get the glass, (not yet completely drained) out of her hands. She battles with him, trying to hit him on the head with a stone. He finally wrests the glass away, though it breaks in his hand, cutting him in the process.*

### RO (v.o.)
**...and maybe you, too, in the process!...**

---

361.    EXT. SAME SIGHT. On Ro, staring disgustedly O.S. There is a
SOUND of retching- Kelly, of course, throwing up nearby.

**RO**
**By now it ought to be plain,- want to lose the baby, you're
going to have to get rid of yourself first.**

CAMERA PULLS BACK to reveal Kelly, pale, wan, crawling back near
the fire. She glares. Still breathing painfully, recovering.

**RO**
**The whole thing is just dumb, what's it worth dead? Nothing!
Alive, you could at least get some mileage out of it. There are
plenty of people...**

*She still doesn't answer. Relentlessly silent. He takes a piece of paper
from his notebook, and a pen.*

361.  Cont.

**RO**
**Look, I'll write you an I.O.U. myself.**
(after scribbling a few lines on paper, looking back up)
**No more death-wish vaudeville- We'll locate a place for you to stay
cheap. And after your time comes, you'll sell me the merchandise-
wholesale. And walk off with the money, free and clear...**

*He writes. She stares at him uncomprehending, utterly bewildered,
unrelentingly silent. He hands her the scrawled piece of paper. He has
to urge it on her, she is reluctant to make the contact even.*

**RO**
**Ordinary business arrangement. Happens every day.** He moves to
examine her ankle. She glares, resists.

**RO**
(*calmly*)
**C'mon. You're carrying my "investment," man has a right to
protect his "investment." Okay?**
*He bends over, checking her bandaged ankle. She looks at him,-not
understanding quite, allowing him nevertheless .*

151

DISSOLVE:

---

362.     SAME SIGHT- MUCH LATER- by the firelight. ON Kelly, RATHER CLOSE. She is huddled up, writing fiercely in a large scrapbook , which she shields from outside view ,a scrapbook which is never out of her grasp. CAMERA SLOWLY PANS AWAY from her, and over to Ro seated calmly, in the Lotus gazing at the girl- his expression a peculiar mixture of aggravation and unwilling, even paternal, concern.

### RO (v.o.)
**I told myself -later when she's asleep - I might have a peek inside that notebook, find somebody to "notify"...**

DISSOLVE:

---

363.     *SAME SIGHT- MUCH LATER AT NIGHT. The fire has died down. Kelly is sleeping , her scrapbook next to her. Ro slowly crawls over, and stealthily picks it up.*

### RO (v.o.)
**A lie, of course. What I really wanted , I'm, afraid...**

*He has now opened her diary, and begins to read.*

### RO (v.o.)
**...was to go on indulging my weakness for recording the secrets of other peoples' lives!**

364.     CLOSE- PART OF SCRAPBOOK PAGE- showing picture of a hip character with guitar, long hair. Kelly with him. Standing outside amusement park photo booth. Her blouse is open; she has nothing on, obviously , underneath.

### KELLY (v.o.)
**"I really love him, his name is Vincent. He has all the records of the Rolling Stones. But we can't make it, unless we're in danger of being caught, like inside a photo booth or something..."**

365.    ANOTHER PHOTO IN SCRAPBOOK, a white girl, in slacks,
very severe. Together with Kelly on a boardwalk .

### KELLY (v.o.)

379.              *ROAD- DAWN.  ON A JEEP moving slowly down the
road, in the New Mexican mesa country; it is painted black. It
seems to have been altered from some reason; in white letters
on one side are the letters LF-SW. The jeep is moving down the
road, CAMERA MOVING with it, SLOWLY.  It passes Ro, just
as he comes up from the bluff, standing uncertainly for a
second. CAMERA HOLDING ON JEEP, moving past and losing
Ro. The jeep stops . Then deliberately, slowly, begins to back
up.  It finally comes back INTO SHOT with Ro, and stops.  He
looks at it, bewildered. FOUR MEN get out suddenly. They are
all blacks. They all have sub-machine guns. They are all
wearing guerilla-like berets and clips of bullets, and crude
insignia, with the same letters as the ones on the jeep. They
surround Ro in a twinkling . Their faces have no expressions;
they are holding four tommy guns on him.*

### RO
Hey, what's happening...I mean, if you're after some bread, then-

There is, apparently, a transistorized speaker
somewhere inside the jeep.

### JEEP SPEAKER
(*very loud*)
Where are you headed?

Ro hesitates.

### JEEP SPEAKER
(*continuing*)
Answer!

### RO
Santa Fe...

### JEEP
Alone?

### RO
Yes ...

379.  Cont.

**<u>JEEP</u>**
**State following : Name, age, occupation?**

**<u>RO</u>**
**Thirty. Student. Rowen Williams ...**
**But look -**

**<u>JEEP</u>**
**Next of kin?**

**<u>RO</u>**
**...Mrs. Emily Williams .**

<u>JEEP</u>
**Living where?**

**<u>RO</u>**
**Two one three Rathborn Street,**
**Washington, D.C....**

**<u>JEEP</u>**
**Okay.  Down on your knees!**

Ro hesitates.

**<u>JEEP</u>**
*(continuing)*
**I said -on your knees!**

*One of the bereted blacks shoves Ro to his knees, takes out a stamp pad and a stamp, stamps Ro's forehead deliberately , and returns implement to his pocket. The stamp is of a snarling, familiar black panther- Ro's forehead  has now been branded.*

**<u>JEEP</u>**
**Military order number three one four.  Fanon regiment.**
**Liberation forces. Southwest.**

380.     CLOSE- ON Ro, listening. He can't believe it. It's incredible. The brand glares at us from his forehead .

380.  Cont.

**<u>JEEP (v.o.)</u>**
**Hostage Rowen Williams:**

you are to be executed today at approximately ...
(*obviously looking up the time*)
...oh-seven-one-three hours.  In reprisal for...

381.    *CLOSE- ON Kelly nearby.  She is listening.  Her chest heaves.*
*Undergoing a terrific struggle with herself.  Terrified.*

### JEEP (v.o.)
...the killing yesterday in El Paso, Texas, of three brother
Freedom Fighters by the Fascist Militia of Lodi County...

382.    WHOLE ROADSIDE SCENE- featuring Ro in F.G. -still
surrounded by the bereted blacks, tommy guns in hand.

### JEEP
...in accordance with LF Policy of maintaining a ratio of ten whites
executed for every black man murdered, degraded, or mutilated by
any white colonialist police agency!
(*rather official*)
...Next of kin will be notified by registered mail.  Repeat:  next
of kin will be notified -

### KELLY (v.o.)
No!

383.    ON KELLY- hobbling up the bluff, painfully, furious, hysterical.
CAMERA MOVING with her, as she ENTERS SHOT.

### KELLY
(*screaming* )
Leave him alone, crazy mother-fuckers!

*She hobbles up to stand in front of Ro, still on his knees.*
*She's now beyond caution.*

### KELLY
(*continuing* )
You've got no right!  Who the hell do you think you are!
(*hollering*)
Help!  Somebody! ...Please...
*Suddenly the jeep opens from the top. Few heads pop out, grinning.*
*They are white; one with black horn- rimmed glasses, holding a movie*
*camera; the other holds a mike. The one in horn-rimmed glasses is a*
*director . And this is one of his most triumphant moments.*

## DIRECTOR
### Beautiful!  Oh man!  Gorgeous!

*He gets out of the jeep, together with his assistant. CAMERA MOVING them over to Ro and Kelly, who simply stare, paralyzed. Ro still on his knees, Kelly in front of him.*

## DIRECTOR
*(to his assistant)*
### See what I mean, Roscoe?
### We could rehearse week after week, never come close - right?
*(to Ro and Kelly)*
### Relax, kiddos, you've just been part of a film.  I mean, we're really and truly beholden to you. Here, give them some bills, Roscoe...

*His assistant hands money to Kelly, who takes it ,dumbly.
Still not quite comprehending .*

## DIRECTOR
*(continuing)*
### Oh man!  Really fan-tas-tic!

*Director and assistant get back into jeep , followed by the four black men, who never change expression once. The jeep rolls away and O.S. Ro still on his knees, benumbed.   Kelly standing in front of him, her belly at the level of his face.*

## KELLY
### Sons of bitches! Crazy mother-fucking sons of bitches!

383.  Cont.
She looks down at Ro. Suddenly , in a maternal gesture she        grabs his head to her belly, cries. Her tears are mostly silent. In a sudden gesture of revulsion, Ro flings his tape recorder, hanging    from one shoulder, away, down the bluff. CAMERA ZOOMS IN, HOLDS on his forehead, pressed against Kelly's life-filled belly: the stigma of the branded panther glaring ...Simultaneously we HEAR the brief continued ticking of the Curie counter for a few more instants, racing slightly faster than before. FREEZE SCENE

# AQUARIUS

## "DON'T BE AFRAID TO
## LOOK INTO THE DEPTHS!"

384.  EXT. SOUTH RIM GRAND CANYON- LATE AFTERNOON. ON
      Nicholas, staring; he looks very ragged, unshaven. He holds a
      dog-eared telegram in one hand. His eyes show no sleep for
      several days.

                        CAROL (v.o.)
                 **Please, daddy, be sensible .**

CAMERA PULLS BACK to show his daughter, Carol,
standing next to him.

                           CAROL
              **If we went to the authorities ...?**

                         NICHOLAS
                           **No!**

385.  REVERSE ANGLE: the incredible cavern of the Grand

      Canyon, from THEIR POV. CAMERA SLOWLY PANNING, to

      illustrate their moving field of vision.

                        CAROL (v.o.)
            **But we don't even know she's still around!.. .**

386.  Carol and Nicholas slowly walking along the south rim, behind
      its official abutment.

                           CAROL
                **I mean, the telegram was vague.**
              **And after all, I got it two days ago?..**

                         NICHOLAS
                         **She's here!**

387.  MOVING- the Canyon itself. The fantastic, implausible mystery-
      beyond-mysteries of the Canyon. Indescribable. People are
      passed, frozen in awestricken attitudes.

                        CAROL (v.o.)
          **But the lodge said they hadn't seen her since morning?**

388.  TWO SHOT- Nicholas and Carol.
      As the two of them look around.

### NICHOLAS
Look, let's not argue. You go that way, I'll go straight ahead...

388.  Cont.

### CAROL
Daddy?

He looks at her for a second.

### CAROL
(*continuing*)
I mean, I still don't get it.  Was she running away?  From what?

### NICHOLAS
I don't know...
(*simply*)

*He moves on, CAMERA losing Carol, staying on Nicholas; in spite of himself he can't help noticing the great gorge.*

### MECHANICAL SLOT-MACHINE GUIDE (v.o.)
(*very metallic*)
" -called by the Indians, Sipapu, the place of emergence. And the canyon itself, - the Mountain Around Which Moving Was Done...

389.  GROUP OF TOURIST ,transfixed , listening to this gadget. As Carol comes by, carefully checking faces, seeing nobody recognizable .

### MECHANICAL GUIDE
...statistically:  three miles thick, one mile deep, two hundred and seventeen miles long...

390.  RATHER LONG -INTO THE indescribable depths of the canyon.

### MECHANICAL GUIDE (v.o.)
...the whole history of man- a brief million years- is only a tiny space down, of course...

391.  SLOW PAN- ON awestruck tourists' faces, still peering over the edge.

**...the rock walls are a calendar of inconceivable time, going back hundreds of millions of years to the ...**

391.  Cont.

A ROAR of jet planes fleetingly blots out the sound.

392.    ANOTHER ANGLE . Onto the walls of the canyon.

### MECHANICAL GUIDE (v.o.)
**...and on the bottom, great vertical layers of gneiss, formed even before the planet itself had cooled...**

393.    EXT. ROAD NEARBY- MOVING- ON Nicholas.  He is walking down toward a SOUND ahead of him, OUT OF CAMERA. We HEAR a jingling and jangling, Indian chanting. He begins to come on the ragged edges of parked cars, people standing ,some sitting .

394.    *CENTER OF INDIAN DANCE AREA- SIDE OF THE ROAD.  A COWBOY with a hand mike standing, an old barker. A group of rather shabby tourist dance Indians stand beside him. A small bonfire has been lit. The Indians are painted and jangled . One is a small child, who comes forward with his tambourine, in which people are placing coins .*

### BARKER
**Thank you, folks . We thank you very kindly...**

395.    *ON Nicholas- moving- beginning to search through the dense watching crowd .*

### BARKER (v.o.)
**"and now for our next presentation- Chief Buffalo Horn's group is going to chant and dance part of Flint Way, one of the great annual Navaho ceremonials ..."**

396.    CROWD OF FACES- A SLOW PAN- FROM NICHOLAS' SEARCHING POV.

### BARKER (v.o.)
**...which usually takes five days and four nights to perform...incidentally, Flint has always been sacred to the Indians, you know...**

397.    ON Ro and Kelly. They are standing near her parked
        motorcycle, watching.  Flames on their faces. He has his arm
        about her; her belly sticks out in the dying light.

397.  Cont.
### BARKER (v.o.)
**...since it's derived from the source of all life, the sun itself. And
the real purpose of this dance is a sort of restoration of life and
vitality, - to keep the sun on our side, you might say...**

398.    ON Nicholas- moving- getting more despairing. He passes
        INTO SHOT with Ro and Kelly. He doesn't know them,
        of course. He pushes on, CAMERA HOLDING on him,
        losing them.

### BARKER (v.o.)
**...after all, we palefaces mustn't forget that we're all sun
worshippers ourselves. In fact, it's only a little ways from here...**


Nicholas stops suddenly, riveted in his tracks, after recognizing his
own wife, Helen, standing not fifteen feet away! He is pierced by a guilty
realization that his self-chosen role as a teacher --- to his own
parishioners say, who couldn't care less about hearing (mystifying)
fables extracted from selected wise men, -- up to and including the
inexcusable spectacle of the city's expanding homeless population,
sleeping these days in public rest rooms, old cars, under park benches,
and nearby alleyways etc., until abruptly woken up—under orders of the
Mayor, - by stern-faced cops who first frisk them for drugs, then order
them sternly to move on.... ----All of which---especially his angry
protests on behalf of the homeless in the local paper-- must have
bothered his dear wife  more  than he knew— to judge  by her sudden,
spontaneous (and near disastrous!)  flight ---which, he never saw
coming, and, which obviously, now demands a more frank --and long
overdue---conversation  among themselves, which could end up (though
he prays it won't!) turning into a painful life-changer, for each one of
them!


### BARKER (v.o.)
**...not so long ago that we first learned to sense its real power
-something the Indians have always intuited –especially after the
exploded, at Alamagordo, New Mexico, the month of July 1945.**

399.    ON Helen. Standing away at the edge of the crowd watching,
        rapt. She seems strangely detached, yet enraptured.  A thin

shawl over her shoulders. She is cradling a small black cat in her arms. Fire projects its geometric evanescence on her face, increasingly lit up, as the blaze gets higher.

The SOUND, O.S., of the Indians strange, melancholy, guttural chant begins, a diachronic monotone. The bells, the cries, the tambourines; the thudding of bare feet on the earth. BUILDS. And as it builds, the CAMERA , HOLDING HELEN squarely in view, ZOOMS CLOSER and closer She becomes bigger and bigger, until, finally her face disappears, entirely, and only the tiny innocent shrinking animal clutched in her arms is IN FOCUS. This, too, enlarges to nearly fill the screen.
FREEZE FRAME.

Against the increasing outcry of the ongoing (showbiz) Indian ceremonial, with its chants and jangles and bare thudding feet; there is the sudden familiar sound of the Curie counter, barely discernable against the ritual dance itself and fading away.

The RATTLE suddenly CEASES. Superimposed suddenly beneath the eyes of the cat, is the same legend with which the film began.


399. Cont.

**"ARE WE TO HAVE A CHANCE TO LIVE?**

**WE DON'T ASK FOR PROSPERITY OR EVEN SECURITY.**

**ONLY FOR A REASONABLE CHANCE TO LIVE, TO WORK OUT**

**OUR DESTINY IN PEACE AND DECENCY..."**


George Wald, MD

Nobel Prize, Medicine,---1968

****

HOLD for a long minute in utter SILENCE. The enigmatic eyes of the cat are fleetingly visible: harbinger of who knows what kinds of eventual mischief may have been,-- though inadvertently,-- already set afoot.

# FADE OUT

162

# About the Author

Alan Marcus has been a professional writer since 1946. He is a novelist (Straw to Make Brick and Of Streets and Stars), a short story writer (Atlantic "first" winner, annual O'Henry collection honors), award-winning playwright (Pity For the Blind), and distinguished radio dramatist (The Peabody Award-winning program, "The Eternal Light"). He is a former Guggenheim Fellow and ex-foreign correspondent accredited to both The Nation and The Atlantic Monthly.

Please address all queries, comments, and requests for further information to OtherShorePress@prodigy.net

# REQUIEM

The crucified planet Earth,
should it find its voice and a sense of irony,
might now well say of our abuse of it,
Forgive them, Father, They know not what they do.

The irony would be that we knew very well
what we were doing  !!

And when the last living thing has died on account of us,
how poetical might it   be
if Earth might then say,
in a voice floating up ,perhaps
from the floor
of the Grand Canyon,

It is done."

Apparently, people did not like it here.

--Kurt Vonnegut

Proof

Made in the USA
Charleston, SC
01 May 2015